"Luke," she said softly. Her lips lifted with the hint of a hopeful smile.

For a second, he was tempted to take her into his arms and hold her, comfort her, try to erase the worry and anguish embedded in her expression. But then his attention flicked to her companion—the boy—and a different heartache overwhelmed him.

He looked so much like Brandon that it hurt.

Grief, guilt and bone-deep regret stabbed him in the heart. The urge to run washed over him. The urge to run from this reckoning. But he couldn't run. He could only hobble. So he did.

"Excuse me," he said, as he pushed past her and made his way blindly down the street—as though they'd never met, as though he'd never loved her from afar, as though she'd never married his best friend.

As though Luke hadn't been responsible for her husband's death.

Dear Reader,

Welcome to book three of the Stirling Ranch series, where our hero, Luke Stirling, returns home after several tours of duty overseas and devastating injuries from an IED. The problem is, as the black sheep of the family, the one who never fit in and never measured up, it doesn't feel very much like home to him.

Luke's story has a double-edged emotional sword for me. As an army brat, I have had an insider's view of what it's like to be in a military family as well as some of the challenges soldiers can come home with after fighting in combat. Survivor's guilt is a huge part of that.

For Luke, the guilt is even more brutal because one of the buddies he lost in that IED explosion was his best friend, Brandon Stoker. When Luke comes face-to-face with Brandon's widow and the son who looks too much like him for comfort, will he be able to overcome the guilt to make peace with his past?

Aside from that, Luke is dyslexic. He understands how to cope with this challenge, but when he was a kid, it alienated him from the world. When Luke learns that Brandon's son, Jack, is dyslexic as well, and that Luke can help Jack, he has a new choice to make. Face up to the challenge—or run.

I'd like to share with you that I, too, am dyslexic—and proud to show the world that learning challenges are just that. Challenges. We can overcome them.

Please check out all my books and contests on sabrinayork.com, and if you want to get updates about future books and tiara giveaways—and snag a free book—sign up for my newsletter at sabrinayork.com/gift.

Happy reading, my darlings!

Sabrina York

The Marine's Reluctant Return

SABRINA YORK

HARLEQUIN
SPECIAL EDITION

Recycling programs
for this product may
not exist in your area.

ISBN-13: 978-1-335-40838-9

The Marine's Reluctant Return

Copyright © 2022 by Sabrina York

This edition published by arrangement with Harlequin Books S.A.

For questions and comments about the quality of this book, please contact us at CustomerService@Harlequin.com.

Harlequin Enterprises ULC
22 Adelaide St. West, 41st Floor
Toronto, Ontario M5H 4E3, Canada
www.Harlequin.com

Printed in U.S.A.

Sabrina York is the *New York Times* and *USA TODAY* bestselling author of hot, humorous romance. She loves to explore contemporary, historical and paranormal genres, and her books range from sweet and sexy to scorching romance. Her awards include the 2018 HOLT Medallion and the National Excellence in Romantic Fiction Award, and she was also a 2017 RITA® Award nominee for Historical Romance. She lives in the Pacific Northwest with her husband of thirty-plus years and a very drooly Rottweiler.

Visit her website at sabrinayork.com to check out her books, excerpts and contests.

This book is dedicated to my brave readers who never give up trying to make the world a better place.

Chapter One

Luke Stirling awoke in a terror—skin clammy, heart pounding, an old nightmare echoing in his brain. It took a moment, longer than it should have, for him to catch his breath, to realize where he was. To know that he was safe.

Safe.

Yet the shadows looming in the dark corners chilled his blood.

With a panicked motion, he turned on the bed lamp and strafed the room with a preternaturally sharp gaze, taking in every nook and cranny. He even looked under the bed, though he knew, logically, there was nothing there. Still, he had to make sure.

That was the ugly thing about fear. It didn't operate on any commonly understood logic or reasoning. It was a terror that rose from the emptiness of the night, preying on his memories, creating monsters where there were none.

It had been three years since the horrible day when he'd lost his team to an IED in Afghanistan. He was back in good old Butterscotch Ridge. Had been for nearly a year. When were the nightmares going to stop?

Well, one thing was for sure. He was done sleeping for the night. He'd had this experience enough to know better than to try. He tossed back the covers and slowly levered his body into a seated position, grimacing as tight muscles and aching joints screamed. The pain was always worse in the morning.

He sucked in a deep breath and forced himself to push through the stretches of his morning routine. As always, he had to remind himself, through the discomfort, that he was lucky. Lucky that his legs moved at all. Lucky they were still attached to his body. Lucky there was breath in his lungs.

So many of his fellow United States Marines had come home with much, much less. If they'd returned at all.

After warming up enough, he stood. The first effort failed and he plopped down on the bed again. By the third try, he was stable enough to walk the short distance to the bathroom. He didn't look in the mirror as he washed his face and brushed his teeth; even though he kept a little scruff to cover most of the damage, he still hated seeing his reflection. And who could blame him?

The IED had not been kind.

The scars he'd sustained on his face were bad enough. But the ones on his left flank? Even he could barely stand to look at them. There were all kinds of puckers and pits where shrapnel had torn thorough his flesh. They ran over his arm, down his side and spattered his hip. Farther down his thigh, there was one long, ragged scar, where the doctors had set the multiple breaks in his legs with titanium posts.

He shook his head, as though to dislodge these thoughts. He hated thinking about his body anymore.

By the time he was dressed—and had eaten a microwaved breakfast sandwich and had a cup of joe—he felt better. He dropped into the chair by the window and checked his schedule for the day. He was glad to see it was a busy one. He liked being busy. He liked being useful.

While he worked at the family ranch when his injuries allowed—though his siblings hardly needed his help—he especially liked helping his fellow vets living in the church-run homeless shelter. Because there, he felt like he *mattered*.

Granted, he didn't do anything life-changing as a now-and-again handyman for the church and its shelter, which was a converted motel that had failed sometime in the nineties because people rarely came to this small town in Washington State on purpose. But sometimes, when a person was hurting, just having someone else around who'd walked in their boots could be really powerful medicine.

And even if none of the other vets needed him, *he* needed *them*. For exactly the same reason.

He drew in a deep breath as he stepped outside the little house he rented in the older part of town. He loved early mornings like this. They reminded him of going fishing with his grandfather when he was a little boy, sitting on the edge of the lake in a cool cloak of misty silence next to the man he admired most.

But that had been long ago, back when the old man had adored him too. Before Luke had started school, and everything had changed.

There was a mist clinging to the trees, a delicate veil making the run-down neighborhood seem almost mystical. Even the spider webs were beautiful, speckled with glinting dewdrops reflecting the rising sun. A cool breeze drifted by. Crickets chirped, and frogs chirruped down by the nearby pond as he made his way across the baseball field to the church. The grass made his shoes damp and he smiled, reminded of a more innocent time.

A light was on in the rectory kitchen, so he knocked, softly.

Suzie Sweet opened the door with a warm smile. But then, Reverend Sweet's wife always smiled. "Good morning, Luke," she said, wiping her hands on a dish towel. "Goodness, you're up early. Couldn't sleep again?"

He forced a grin. "Just can't wait to get to work, I guess."

She saw through him. She always did. "You work too hard."

"I like to keep busy, ma'am."

"Of course, you do. Have you had breakfast?" He nodded and she narrowed her eyes. "Real food, I mean."

"I'm good. Thank you."

"Some coffee?"

"Actually, I'd like to get started with the heater." Though it was only October, a cold wind was coming down from the north.

She nodded. "That would be nice. No one's looking forward to sitting through this week's sermon in an icebox. Oh… Luke?"

"Yes, ma'am?"

"Would you be willing to look at the kitchen sink when you're done? I think something's stuck in the drain."

"Sure thing, ma'am."

"You are a dear." That smile again. "Oh. I made some cookies for you and the guys." She waved to a Tupperware container on the counter.

He couldn't hold back a grin. He loved her cookies, and so did the other vets. "That's really thoughtful, ma'am. Thank you."

Suzie handed him the keys to the church and sent him on his way, but she insisted he take a muffin with him before she'd let him leave.

Luke was glad for the muffin when the heater turned out to be a bear to fix. It was midmorning before he finally got it to work. He'd been trained as a mechanic in the military—as well as other things—and he enjoyed being able to use his skills to make life easier for the people he cared about. But not because he fancied himself a *good person*, whatever that was. He just saw each and every opportunity to help others as a way to cosmically thumb his nose at the old man. *Guess I'm not so useless after all, am I?*

He snorted to himself. Funny how quickly things could go bad, wasn't it? One day, he and the old man had been closer than two peas in a pod. And the next…his grandfather was railing about how inadequate he was. And Luke had been reminded he was less than perfect more than once. More than once a day, actually, if memory served. Tough thing to take, for a six-year-old. Would it have made any difference, he wondered, if the old man had understood what dyslexia was? Or had taken the time to learn about it for himself? To realize that Luke wasn't lazy or stupid?

Probably not. Some people, he'd discovered, just enjoyed finding fault.

Some people, he'd discovered, should be avoided like the plague.

After he finished the heater, Luke started on the rectory kitchen sink. As the day was going, that was a bear, too. Someone had, indeed, clogged the pipe. With a wash rag, of all things. This required him to crawl into the musty cabinet underneath the sink and dismantle the pipes.

It didn't take long at all, but before he could finish, he was interrupted.

"Hey, Dummy. Zat you?"

Luke froze in the process of tightening a bolt at the sound of a too-familiar voice—a too-familiar slur he'd thought had been relegated to the past. Irritation raised the hairs on the back of his neck. Something acidic rose in his throat. No one had called him *Dummy* in years. Not since he'd left this godforsaken town. But here *he* was again. Trent Cooper, picking at old scabs.

Of all the people Luke had avoided since returning home, Trent was at the top of the list—well, pretty damn close to the top of the list—and for damn good reason. Oh, they'd seen each other. Usually from across a crowded bar. But neither of them had made any attempts to reach out. Certainly not to *talk*.

Which was totally fine.

What surprised Luke was how quickly that old bitterness arose in his soul. Just those few words and he was that angry kid again. Had he really thought he'd *evolved*? Had he really thought anything had changed around here? That it ever would?

He sucked in a deep breath and prepared to disentangle himself from beneath the sink. Lying flat on his back, helpless, was no way to face one's old nemesis. But just as he was pulling himself up, the tip of Trent's boot smacked Luke's jean-clad thigh and his body seized in response. Heat prickled his skin, sweat beaded on his brow. Pain, sharp as a blade, sliced through him, setting his nerves on fire. He shot up and smacked his forehead on the drainpipe.

Son of a bitch. That hurt.

When the blinding agony abated, along with the rushing in his ears, Luke heard it. Trent's laugh.

Was it irony that Trent had managed to zero in on the exact spot that hurt the most? Or just a lot of practice? Trent had always been an ass—the town bully, like his father before him. A prodigy. His barbs rarely missed their mark. He was one of the reasons Luke had left this Podunk town.

Back then, Luke had vowed to find a way to prove himself to everyone. To show them he wasn't as worthless as everyone seemed to think. But, more importantly, he'd vowed to find his place in the world. And he had. He'd become his own man.

He hadn't expected that hard-won peace would be so damn difficult to hang on to.

With another deep breath, he fought down his rising temper. It had taken a long time for him to address, confront and master his issues from the past. It had been a long, hard fight, but he'd won. And he wasn't going to let his bitterness own him again.

"You comin' out of there?" Trent asked. Thank God he didn't nudge Luke again with that damn boot. The injury in his thigh was particularly sensitive today—which meant it was probably going to rain.

In response, Luke slid out from under the sink and stood.

Was it wrong to feel that little tingle of satisfaction as his old bully's gaze flicked higher, and higher yet, to meet his? Was it wrong to feel a little smug when Trent took in his new physique—molded by his years in the service—and his jaw dropped? Yeah. Luke wasn't a stupid, helpless boy anymore. He was a man.

And…had Trent always been that short?

Luke had known returning home might mean facing his old demons again—he just hadn't expected it to be *this* challenging. He didn't throw a punch, but only because Suzie Sweet wouldn't approve. Also, he reminded himself, he wasn't that easily insulted hothead anymore.

Aside from that, it wouldn't be a fair fight—not

that Trent had ever cared about what was fair. Since Luke left town—eight years ago—he'd been trained in multiple forms of lethal combat. He'd mastered strategy and tactics, psychology, mechanics, operations, logistics, aviation and more.

Not to mention the fact that he had a solid forty pounds of muscle on Trent, who had, apparently, grown some love handles.

Oh, yeah. Luke could take him. One good punch would probably do it.

But Luke wasn't a raging hormone anymore, ready to flail wildly at anyone and everyone who slighted him in any way, shape or form. He was a man of honor.

Well, some honor. He had at least a little bit of it left.

"Wow." Trent looked him up and down and then crossed his arms over his chest. A classic defensive move. "Look at your face." Typical bully. Honing in on what he thought was Luke's weakness.

Luke turned on the tap and bent to make sure the sink wasn't leaking. Nope. It was good. He kept looking, though, longer than he needed to, because he didn't want to engage with Trent.

Also, it annoyed Trent to be ignored.

As though in answer to a prayer he hadn't uttered, Suzie Sweet interrupted their tête-à-tête. "How's it going, Luke?" she said as she poked her head into the room with her trademark perky smile. It dimmed when she saw Trent. "Well, hey, Mr. Cooper," she said, taking in his tracksuit. "You coaching today?" The Butterscotch Ridge baseball and soccer fields were nestled between the church and the elementary school, which explained how Trent had found himself this close to the sanctuary. Any closer and he might burst into flames.

Trent nodded. "Gotta keep those kids on the top of their game." He turned to Luke. "I'm coaching soccer. My son's the star player!"

"Is that so?"

"You used to play, didn't you, Stirling?" Oh. Now he was *Stirling*? What happened to Dummy? "You used to be a pretty good runner." His gaze flicked down to Luke's leg. "Back then."

Heat flooded Luke's face. Was that a jab? Another barb to get a reaction from him? Because there was no running in Luke's future, that was for damn sure. He shifted his weight as another bolt of pain shot through his left leg, and he let the silence between himself and Trent swelter for a minute.

Was it wrong to be gratified when Trent flushed and muttered a barely audible, "Sorry"?

"Oh, gracious me. What am I thinking?" Mrs. Sweet interjected when the lack of conversation became too much for her to bear. She really was a nice woman. All she wanted was for everyone to just get along. What a shame she lived in this town. "I promised you a soda, Luke. Did you get that sink all fixed up? And don't forget the cookies."

The soda was great—beer would've been better—and Luke took the cookies, too, because she'd made a special point of making them for the guys.

"I can't tell you how much I appreciate your help," she continued, folding and refolding that kitchen towel, which, if one was being brutally honest, didn't seem to have many folds left in it. "I don't know what we'd have done come Sunday if the heater was out."

Luke smiled. "People'd still come to hear you sing in the choir, Mrs. Sweet," he said, because he knew she prided herself on her dulcet alto.

Naturally, she flushed.

Luke collected all his tools and thanked Mrs. Sweet for the refreshments, figuring this was an appropriate juncture for his escape. It was a damn shame Trent followed him out after saying his own goodbyes.

Was it Luke's imagination, or did the reverend's wife close the door behind Trent a little more firmly than necessary?

Luke headed for home with Trent beside him. Thank God it was only a few blocks away, because his leg was really howling now. Truth be told, he'd probably overdone it this morning. Lately his muscles had been cramping up more and more. It was even starting to affect his work at the ranch. It was irritating as hell. Trent slowed to allow Luke to keep pace with him, but Luke knew better than to assume it was an act of charity. The SOB just wanted to keep needling him.

Sure enough, after a moment of silence, Trent said, "It's nice of the reverend to give you odd jobs. You know, seeing as you're unemployed."

Luke glanced at him and didn't mention that all his work for the church was voluntary. With his military disability pay and savings, along with his stake in the family ranch, he was hardly hurting for money. And he had simple tastes, so he didn't have a lot of expenses. Then again, he didn't need much. Just his little house and a lot of peace and privacy.

Oh, his family griped about his modest living arrangements. "We're the Stirlings," his older brother DJ occasionally reminded him. "We have a reputation to uphold." It was as though he'd never noticed that Luke wasn't perfect like the rest of them. That he felt like the cuckoo in the Stirling nest.

"We can't have the whole town thinking you're not welcome at the ranch," his sister, Samantha, would add in her usual direct way. As if she'd never noticed Luke felt like a lesser soul, even though the old man had made his opinion on this more than clear, bellowing it all through the house whenever grades came in.

For his part, Mark just shrugged his shoulders

and said, "Whatever makes you happy, bro," because that's the way *he* was.

And the old man…

Well, there was no reason to think about him anymore, was there?

His grandfather was dead. The only conversations Luke could have with him now were the ones in his head. Somehow, they still fought.

Funny how one person can have such conflicting feelings about another. Hate someone and love them at the same time. Mostly, what he felt about Daniel Stirling Sr. was regret. Regret that he'd never gotten the chance to show the old bastard the man he'd become.

Oh, he'd flown home the minute he got word that the old man was dying. He'd just arrived too late for that confrontation—the one he'd been dreading for eight years.

"So what do you think?"

Caught by surprise, Luke realized they'd reached his place.

Also, apparently, Trent had been talking.

"Think?" Repeating the last word of a question like this usually worked when he hadn't been paying attention.

"You wanna come play poker with me and the guys tonight?" Trent sent him a grin. Naturally, it made Luke suspicious.

His chest contracted. A myriad of bitter childhood memories of Trent and his minions flooded him.

Not only no, but hell no. "Sorry. I'm busy."

"Oh. Right." Trent's eyes widened. "I get it." *Did he?* "I can spot you the ante if you want."

Luke blinked. Trent thought he couldn't *afford* to play poker with him and his buddies. Well, as excuses went, that one worked. "Yeah. I couldn't do that. But thanks." And with that, he let himself into his house, nodded farewell and shut the door in Trent's face, though he clearly wanted to be invited in.

No thanks. His place was his refuge. A person did not invite an ogre into their refuge.

One thing Luke had learned on his journey was that when he had the ability to avoid unpleasant things, and things that caused him pain, he did. He avoided them like the plague. If that meant shutting the door in Trent Cooper's face, so much the better.

"You got that okay?" Chase McGruder asked Crystal Stoker as she hefted a tray piled with outgoing orders.

She grinned up at him. "Yep." After years of working at the local bar and grill, the Butterscotch Ridge B&G, Crystal was used to balancing things. Lots of things. Still, Chase held open the swinging doors from the kitchen to the restaurant for her.

But then, Chase was like that. He was a great guy and an awesome boss, and he'd embraced Crystal and her son, Jack, in their darkest hour. Three years ago, when her husband, Brandon—Chase's cousin—had died, leaving their little family with no income what-soever, Chase had given her a job. And then, when she lost Grandma's house because she couldn't pay the taxes, he'd let them live in the apartment above the restaurant. Because of him, she was still able to take care of her son. Since both Brandon's and Crystal's parents had died long ago, the McGruders were the only family she and Jack had anymore.

On her way to the back booth, she passed a table of the morning regulars, Al, Johnny P. and Rufus, three of the local vets. "Hey there, sweetheart," Rufus said with a wink. He always flirted with her, even though he was old enough to be her grandfather. Maybe her great-grandfather.

"You need anything, hon?" she asked, scanning their coffee mugs.

"Just your hand in marriage, darling."

"You know I can't cook worth a hill of beans, Rufus."

"But you'd sure look pretty burning the toast," he responded.

She chuckled. "More coffee?"

"You bet."

"I'll be right back with it, as soon as I drop these off."

He lifted his mug in a salute. "I s'pose I'll have to settle for the coffee then," he said with a smile. It was infectious. It always was.

She was still smiling as she handed out the food

to the customers in the back booth, even though the patrons—cheerleader Pam, her BFF, Karen, and Sophia Cage, who was Butterscotch Ridge's answer to Khloe Kardashian—were all girls she'd gone to high school with, way back when. Oh, they hadn't been friends, and they still weren't, but that didn't matter. This was only a job. A way to put food on the table for her son. "Can I get you anything else?" she asked when the tray was empty.

Pam sent her something of a smirk. "This fork is dirty."

"Sure. I'll get you another. Right away." The fork was spotless. Pam always asked for random things. Probably because she liked being waited on, and this was the only place in town to offer that luxury. "Anyone else need anything?" she asked, but the others were too glued to their phones to answer.

After she brought Pam another table setting, and topped up Rufus and his buddies, she headed for the kitchen to get a drink of water. Though the restaurant was air-conditioned, Crystal was very aware of the dabs of sweat on her uniform. It was probably all the running around. But she couldn't complain about that, because being this busy helped her keep fit. It was why she always wore track shoes to work.

"Hey, Crystal?" Chase poked his head into the kitchen as she tipped back her chilled water bottle. She liked to measure it out in the morning, to make sure she kept herself hydrated. Once the day started, it was "go, go, go." So different than life had been when Brandon had been alive. "You've got a phone call." His tone made clear it wasn't good news.

Crystal's stomach twanged. She sighed and wiped her hands on her apron. "Who is it?" she asked. As if she didn't know.

"Stella Anders."

Yup. Crap. "Okay."

"Take it at the bar."

Double crap. The last thing she needed was witnesses. But still, she kept a smile on her face as she made her way to the bar phone. "Hello, Mrs. Anders. What's up?" Even though they'd known each other forever—Stella was the local school principal—Crystal always called her "Mrs. Anders," so Jack would understand what it meant to respect his elders. Sometimes she wondered if she'd failed to make that point.

"Crystal." Stella's voice was tight and clipped. "I'm sorry to bother you at work, but we have a problem."

We? Crystal knew the problem was all hers. It always was. Her gut clenched and more sweat prickled on her brow. She turned her back on the bar patrons, who were blatantly listening in. "Mmm-hmm?"

"Crystal, Jack got into another fight. I'm sorry, but I'm going to have to send him home again."

She keeps saying she's sorry. Why is she doing that?

"I see." With a soft sigh, Crystal closed her eyes

and leaned against the cool wall. She didn't know what was going on with her son, and every time she tried to ask him why he kept getting into so many fights, he refused to talk to her about it. "I'll come and pick him up. Thanks."

Damn. Crystal raked back her hair, which had somehow wormed its way out of her ponytail. Tears of frustration pricked at her lids, so she hurried back to the kitchen, where there was at least some privacy. Not that anything was a secret in this town. By supper, everyone would know that Jack Stoker had been kicked out of school *again*.

Still, it wasn't the disruption to her day, or the humiliation of having a devil child in a small town, that frustrated her. It was the fact that Jack, her sweet, adorable baby boy, was drifting away from her. Something was wrong with him, and she had no idea what it was.

Some said, "Well, this happens when boys turn eight." And others insisted, "He needs a man around the house." Some even suggested military school.

The hard truth was that three years ago, Jack's dad had died. One day they were chatting on Skype from halfway around the world, and the next day, silence. Deafening silence. Was it any surprise the boy was in pain?

A heavy hand fell on her shoulder and she jumped.

"You okay?" Chase asked.

Crystal nodded, blew her nose and cleared her throat. "I need to go."

"I figured."

"I'll be back as soon as I can."

"I know. We can flip shifts if you need to." He gave her a sideways hug, and she turned it into a full one. To thank him for being so understanding, and also because she really needed a hug. Then she took off her apron, grabbed her keys and headed out the back door to her 2001 Saturn. Brandon had bought the used vehicle for her as a wedding present, and it still worked like a champ. Thank God. The last thing she needed right now was a car payment on top of everything else.

It was a really pretty day, she thought as she drove to the elementary school, but the deep blue skies and fluffy white clouds did nothing to ease her dread. If Jack got suspended again, she would need to pay for childcare while she worked. Worse than that, word had gotten around about Jack. No one wanted to babysit him. Not even Barbara Sue, the most avaricious teenager in town. And Chase's wife, Bella? After Jack "accidently" set her garden shed on fire? Not even a consideration.

Even though they lived in the apartment above Crystal's workplace, the thought of leaving her son there alone all day gave her the heebie-jeebies. Especially after the toaster fire he'd started last week.

It was hard enough being a single mother without any of this.

The tears pricked at her lids again and she brushed them away. It was wrong to point that anger at her dead husband. She knew it was. But sometimes, that's just where it went. If he hadn't followed his best friend into the marines... If he hadn't gone to Afghanistan... If he hadn't died in an explosion on the other side of the world... Everything would be different now.

But those thoughts were pointless. So was self-pity. She sucked in a breath and straightened her spine as she pulled into the parking lot. Jack was there, waiting for her, with Mrs. Anders, who, frankly, looked tired.

"Thank you," Crystal said, as she took her son's hand. Then she added, "I'm so sorry," because she figured both sentiments were germane to this situation. Both were equally mortifying.

Mrs. Anders nodded. "We'll need to talk." Her gaze flicked to Jack. "Later."

Crystal's throat locked. "Um, sure." Not a conversation she was looking forward to. She was pretty sure how it would go. "You ready to go home, sweetie?" she asked her son.

He sent her a sullen look, then stomped to the car.

She sighed and followed, but once she was in the car, she didn't start it. "Do you want to talk about it?" she asked.

He turned to the window. His profile, so precious to her, reminded her of Brandon, when he'd been eight.

"Jack? What happened?"

He tightened his jaw. "Nothing."

"You got in a fight over nothing?"

He shrugged. "I guess."

She knew that truculent expression. She knew peppering him with questions wouldn't help. She just hoped that something could. And she prayed she could discover what it might be. Soon. Because she didn't know what was happening to her son and she had no idea how to help him.

She'd never felt more helpless, or so alone, in her life.

The second Luke was sure Trent had gone, he headed for the record player he kept on a side table in his small living room, as he usually did when he needed some peace. It was a really old thing in a scarred wooden box. He'd picked it up in a thrift store, but as long as he had a good needle, it worked. It even had a jack for his headphones, which he preferred, rather than announcing his musical choices to all and sundry. He flipped through his albums, searching for something that could help him muddle through the ordeal of confronting Trent again. It was one thing seeing him at a safe distance and quite another being close enough to see the gap between his front teeth.

After the IED that had changed his world forever, the one that had taken out the rest of his unit—including his best friend—Luke had gone through all kinds of therapy. Physical, emotional, art therapy. All the tools they used to try and heal the soul of a guy who'd just learned he might never walk again.

The one that had really touched his soul had been music therapy. He had especially gravitated to classical music—the kind he'd never heard before he'd left this town. Somehow, classical music helped him enter that magical place where everything made sense from a structural point of view. No thoughts were required. No words were necessary. It was simply bliss.

It only took a second to find what he was looking for; he unsheathed the vinyl disc from its cover and set it gently on the turntable. His chest warmed at the *pop* as he set the needle on the record. Warmed even more as the first few magnificent notes flooded the room. He quickly plugged in his headphones, collapsed into his chair, closed his eyes and soaked it in.

Nothing about the cello-and-oboe duet took away the guilt, pain and regret he still carried, still felt in every step. But it helped. It soothed him,

The piece had no percussion, so Luke's brow furrowed when an incessant banging intruded his sanctuary. He turned off the music, heaved himself out of his perfectly comfortable chair and stomped to the door.

Swear to God, if it's Trent again—

Ah. But it wasn't Trent. It was Samantha.

Luke turned away from his sister and made a face. She rarely deigned to visit his place since he'd returned home, and he couldn't remember a time she'd actually come inside. Given her opinion about him living here—rather than at the ranch—he knew this encounter would be challenging. Dealing with Sam often was.

Indeed, she peeped inside his compact living room and made a face, though she tried to hide it.

"Come on in," he said dryly. "Hardly any bedbugs."

Her nostrils flared. She reared back. "Bedbugs? Seriously?"

He tipped his head to the side. "You know I'm just messing with you, Sam."

"Don't ever joke about bedbugs. I…" She stepped in and glanced around the living room. "It's not… bad." He nearly snorted. It was like the Hilton, compared to field conditions. As she wandered around, looking at his space and setup, he hoped she could see, now, that he was at home here. Belonged here.

"You've got a microwave," she said from the kitchen, which was also part of the living room/dining room. She sounded surprised.

"Mmm-hmm."

"Nice. And a coffee maker." One of Suzie Sweet's castoffs, because she'd decided she didn't like the pods. "And…" Sam's gaze fell on his record collection and she grinned at him, then started flipping through the albums. Her fingers slowed, then froze. "What is this?" She held up one of his favorites.

"Beethoven."

She arched an eyebrow, then went up on her toes and waggled her fingers. "This is music for fancy folk."

Luke winced. He knew this would be her reaction. He just didn't want to deal with it right now. "It's really not."

"Where's the Slim Whitman?"

Luke snatched the album from her, lest she break it. "It's part of my PT."

"Really?"

Well, kind of. It was certainly therapeutic. It kept him calm. Kept the nightmares at bay. Mostly. "Yep." He diddled a finger around his head. "Classical music rewires the neurons."

"I did not know that. Wow." She nibbled on a fingernail before adding, in a softer voice, "I didn't realize you were still doing therapy."

It was hard to hold back a snort. Some days it felt as though that was all he did. "Healing takes time." He smiled at his sister but didn't mention that it amused to see her off-kilter. She so rarely was. "So what precipitated this visit to the wrong side of the tracks?" he asked.

"You wish there were train tracks in town," she said tartly. Yeah. That was more like her. "I've been meaning to come by and see your place."

"And?" He knew her better than that.

"And I thought I'd take you to the B&G for lunch."

The little hairs on his nape prickled. *The B&G? What day was it? Would she be there?* He checked his phone, then swallowed heavily. It was Friday. Crap. "It's a little late for lunch, isn't it?"

"Is it? It's only one thirty."

Luke made a face. He wasn't exactly hungry, but he knew Sam well enough to know that the easiest thing was just to do what she wanted. "But, why the B&G?" He didn't want to go there. Not today.

Sam snorted through her nose. "I suppose we could go to the other restaurant in town." This, of course, was sarcasm. The B&G was the only restaurant in town, if you didn't count Gram's Book & Bakery, the bookstore/café owned by his brother's girlfriend, Veronica. Who also happened to bake Luke's favorite brownies, hands down.

"Fine." It had been a helluva day already. He could steel his spine and just deal with it. He could ignore her if she were there. Couldn't he? "You ready to go?" he asked brusquely, grabbing his Stetson and jamming it on his head.

"Sure." The fact that her response was all sweet

and nice riled his temper. Sam wasn't "sweet" or "nice." She was a call-'em-like-she-saw-'em real-ist. Her being nice meant she had an agenda. But then, she usually did. She glanced at his leg. "You okay to walk?"

The thought of her pity turned his stomach. He glared at her, mostly because she was still being sweet. "Yeah." For months, that had been his man-tra. *I can walk. I can walk. I can walk.*

"We can always take the truck."

"I can walk, damn it. Come on. I want a beer." But that was a lie. He didn't want a beer. He didn't want to go to the B&G by foot, by truck or be carried there kicking and screaming. And he had a damn good reason.

She worked on Friday afternoons. And honestly, the last thing he needed right now was to see *her* again. He had successfully avoided her for months, just by knowing her schedule—the same way he'd avoided Trent. He'd begun to believe he could avoid her forever.

He should just refuse to go. That's what he should do. But if he did, there would be questions. With his family, there always were. Damn it all, anyway.

He sucked in a breath and stiffened his spine. He was his own man now. He lived his life on his own terms. He didn't owe his family anything. He didn't owe anybody anything—

Wrong.

His heart lurched as his gaze landed on a photograph on the mantel, the one of himself in his high-school football uniform, next to his best friend, Brandon Stoker. He did owe somebody. It was a damn shame he didn't have a clue how to pay back a dead man.

Especially when it was Luke's fault he had died.

Chapter Two

It wasn't far from Luke's place to the bar and grill, but by the time they got there, his entire left flank was howling. There was a tinny taste in his mouth that let him know he'd bit too hard on his cheek again.

He knew he was lucky to be able to walk at all. Right after the explosion, he'd been paralyzed from the waist down. It had been horrifying. The doctors had told him it would take a long time for the neurological and muscular damage to his body to repair itself. Months. Years. And even then, he might not regain full mobility.

Patience had never been his forte. He knew he had to grit his teeth and work through it.

Speaking of gritting his teeth and bearing it… facing Crystal wouldn't be so bad. Would it? He was prepared for it. Wasn't he?

Sam paused and pretended to tie her shoe before they went inside, giving Luke a chance to catch his breath. When they entered the bar, a call went up, just like on *Cheers*. Most of the guys called out to Samantha, but there were a few greetings for him in there, too. Which made him feel good. Then again, he'd been patronizing the B&G on a semiregular basis since he'd returned home.

*Semi*regular because *she* worked every night except Tuesday, Thursday and Friday. He stayed home on the nights she worked. But when did her daytime shift end? Damn it. He didn't know.

His pulse thrummed in his eye as he scanned the restaurant, looking for her. When he didn't see her, a mélange of emotions scudded through him. Surely one of them wasn't regret. Surely he hadn't secretly hoped to see her. He had no business even thinking like that. She'd been his best friend's wife. Still was, as far as Luke was concerned. Yeah, he had no business thinking about her at all.

"Hey, man." Jed Cage came over and slapped his shoulder, mercifully driving almost all thoughts of Crystal from his head. Though the Cages owned the other large ranch close to town—and their grandfathers had been known to feud on occasion—Luke and Jed had always been friendly. "How are you doing, buddy?"

"Great." Sort of true.

"Hey, I heard you're working at the church." Jed raised an eyebrow. "If you need more work—"

"He's not looking for work," Sam said with a sniff. "He's got a job at the ranch. When he feels like showing up." This last bit was directed at Luke in a sarcastic tone on account of the fact he hadn't been to the ranch for a week, because his hip had been acting up something fierce.

Jed chuckled. "Okay. Okay. I was just going to say, we could always use a good hand. You know. If you're interested."

"He's not." Sam took Luke's elbow and tried to steer him to a booth in the back. He hated being steered, mostly because it made it hard to balance, so he resisted.

"Thanks, Jed. I appreciate that." Luke put out his hand and the men shook. That was a damn fine gesture from Jed, and it warmed Luke's heart. Making him feel accepted. It reminded him that not everyone in this town was a jerk like Trent. A reminder that he deeply appreciated. Especially today.

Sam led the way to a booth way back in the corner—she never made anything easy—and sat. Luke tossed his Stetson onto the seat and slid in across from her. A muscle in his thigh seized, and he attempted to massage the knot out without looking like a pervert.

Almost immediately, Chase McGruder, the owner of the B&G, stopped by and dealt out menus like a Vegas blackjack dealer. "Good afternoon," he said in a cheery voice.

"How you doin', Chase?" Luke asked. Though Chase was several years older, he and Luke had always been friendly. Chase had been the kind of guy who didn't like seeing the younger kids get bullied and was more than happy to step in and stop it. He'd stepped in on Luke's account more than once.

"Just peachy." He licked the tip of his pencil. "Can I take y'all's order?"

Sam frowned at him. "Where's Crystal? I need to talk to her about last weekend."

For no reason whatsoever, Luke's heart rate spiked. His gaze snapped to Chase...who shrugged. "She had an errand to run."

A curtain of relief closed on him.

Oh. She wasn't here. Good. That was good.

The reunion he'd been avoiding for months would not happen today. He ignored the little sizzle of disappointment in his gut. It was better this way. It was better if he avoided her. It really was.

As usual, Sam didn't take long to come to the reason she'd dragged him out to lunch. As soon as they had their bacon jam burgers and onion rings, she lit in, outlining all the reasons Luke would be better off living on the ranch. Though he wasn't terribly hungry, Luke appreciated the food, because it gave him a reason not to respond—you know, because his mouth was full and all.

"Are you even listening to me?" Sam asked eventually.

Luke shot her a grin. "Not really." He'd meant it to be a joke, and as such, it fell flat.

She, in fact, deflated, which was a disturbing thing to see. It pierced his heart, because Sam was always the brave one, but he didn't know what to say. Instead he looked away, pretending to study the paintings on the wall, though they'd been there as long as he could remember.

"What happened to you, Luke?" she finally asked in the saddest voice he'd ever heard. He glanced at her and was horrified to see the glint of tears in her eyes. She ignored them—of course, she did—but it was something he just couldn't *un*see.

Heat crawled up his nape. "What do you mean?"

"Come on. Are you trying to tell me you're *not* avoiding me? Avoiding *us*?"

His heart hitched. Had he been? "I don't know what you mean."

"Luke…" He watched her struggle with her thoughts for several moments. "I—I feel like I've lost you."

He forced a laugh. "I'm sitting right here."

"You know what I mean. Since you came back... I don't know. You're...different."

"Lots of men come back changed."

"Lots of men aren't my brother. I miss you. Is it wrong for me to want you back?"

His heart softened, just a little, for her. She was his baby sister, even though she was stronger in spirit and more stubborn than anyone he'd ever met. It was hard to see her like this. Harder still that he couldn't make things better for her.

It had been so easy when she'd been little, with her hair up in pigtails. Back then, a cookie or a piggyback ride and everything was fine.

"I mean, when you first got back, and you said you needed space, room to heal, okay. I got it. But it's been almost a year, Luke."

"Healing doesn't conform to calendars, Sam."

"What about Grandpa's will?"

The will with the codicil added to force his hand? "To hell with the will. To hell with him."

"Or you just don't want to be around us. Is that it?"

She was like a terrier with a bone sometimes. "Sam, you know that's—"

"I just don't understand why you won't move back to the house."

"To *his* house?" He tried not to sound bitter, but it was beyond him.

"So *that's* it." Sam sat back, crossed her arms.

"Grandpa is gone, Luke. It's not his house anymore. You worried he's gonna haunt you?"

Yes. "That's not the point. My memories of that house are dark." A concession, so he wouldn't have to tell her the rest of it.

"We can have it saged." She was probably joking. Burning weeds in the house to clear bad energy would hardly ease his soul-deep discomfort whenever he stepped through the door.

Luke shook his head. He took Sam's hands in his, even though it surprised her and she tried to tug them back. "I'm still healing, Sam." Physically and spiritually. "I need privacy. I need to be alone with myself." And the demons. The demons liked privacy, too, when they howled in the night.

"So live in one of the cabins, like Mark." While Sam, DJ and Grandma lived at the main house, Luke's younger brother lived in one of the crew cabins on the ranch, a stone's throw away.

"I'm not like Mark." Never had been. Not even close. When she didn't respond, he added, "You know it's not personal, right? It's not you or Mark or DJ. It's me."

She frowned. "How cliché." and then, when he didn't respond, "Will you *ever* move back to the house?"

He shrugged. "Don't know." *Probably not.* And they didn't want him to, little did they know. One week of his night terrors—the hollering and thrashing and carrying on—and they'd change their minds. They'd get rid of him quicker than snot on a toddler.

"Will you think about it?"

That, he could promise. "I'll think about it." He released her hand. "But don't go holding your breath, okay?"

She sighed. "All right."

"And Sam?"

"Yes, Luke?"

"It's okay for you to meet me where I am, you know."

Her brow rumpled. "I have no idea what that means."

He chuckled, then sobered when he caught her frown. "Sam, I'm really not *that* Luke anymore. I'm a different guy. Please don't try to change me. You know what they say about putting lipstick on a pig."

"Yes, it annoys the pig. But you're not a pig, Luke. You're my big brother and I—" She paused and re-formed her thought. "I would like to get to know you again." She peeped at him under her lashes. "How's that? Is that okay?"

"Of course, Sam. That's very okay." And the fact that she had *listened* to him, really listened, was even better. It was almost progress. "I'm here. Anytime."

After they finished eating, Sam left the B&G to head back to the ranch, but Luke decided to stay. He told her he wanted to enjoy his beer, but that was a lie. He needed the extra time to get out of the booth, and he didn't want anyone hovering.

When he was finally able to stand, it took a few more moments to get his balance and make his way to the door. *It's just an inconvenience*, he told himself as pain shot through him with every step. *Just an inconvenience.*

He was so focused on his aching thigh as he opened the door that he didn't realize someone was coming in until they were nearly chest-to-chest.

"Sorry," he said automatically, as his brain acknowledged that there was a person blocking his way.

And then, as her scent hit him, his heart stopped.

Then it thudded as he looked into Crystal Stoker's eyes.

A jumble of emotions slammed into him. He stared at her, unable to act or react. Unable to move.

"Luke," she said softly. Her lips lifted with the hint of a hopeful smile.

For a second, he was tempted to take her into his arms and hold her, comfort her, try to erase the worry and anguish imbedded in her expression. But then his attention flicked to the boy at her side, and a different heartache overwhelmed him.

He looked so much like Brandon that it hurt.

Grief, guilt and bone-deep regret stabbed him in the heart. The urge to run consumed him.

"Excuse me," he said, as he pushed past her and

made his way blindly down the street—as though they'd never met, as though he'd never loved her from afar, as though she'd never married his best friend.

As though Luke wasn't the reason her husband was dead.

Crystal's heart went from delight to desolation in a single beat.

Speechless, she stared at Luke Stirling's retreating form. She'd wanted—needed—to see him, to speak to him, since he'd returned to town, but this was not what she had imagined. Not in a million years.

What made things even worse was that she'd suspected he'd been avoiding her, and now she knew for certain. That fact alone crushed her.

"Who was that?" Jack asked, but she couldn't answer. Something clogged her throat.

Finally, she choked out, "He was a friend of your father's."

Her heart ached at her son's expression, as Jack stared after Luke, too.

"Let's go, young man. We need to have a talk." She towed him through the restaurant and the kitchen to the staircase out back that led to their upstairs apartment. It was nothing fancy, but it was enough. There were three bedrooms—one for each of them, and another for her fledgling online business—and a living room/kitchen combo.

As Crystal stepped inside, she took a deep breath, and it calmed her. She'd discovered aromatherapy after Brandon had died. It had saved her sanity to the point that she'd decided to study the skill and then use it to help others when she could, making essential oil-based soaps, lotions and bath bombs. As a result, her apartment was usually a potpourri of beautiful scents, depending on the project at hand. When she wasn't working at the B&G, she took massage clients as well.

Still, even her usual calming ritual didn't work today. It was bad enough that Jack had been in another fight. Now she had to deal with what she could only assume was blatant rejection from the one man she needed right now. The one man who had loved her husband as much as she had. The one man who truly understood her grief.

How could she have imagined that he would greet her with open arms?

"I'm hungry."

Thank God for reality. Jack's complaint brought her right back to the present. "Mac and cheese?" she suggested, because she knew he'd say yes, and it was a brainless meal to make. But because it was, while she fixed his snack, her mind continued to return to Luke Stirling, no matter how hard she tried to think about something else.

She knew why she was obsessed. After losing Brandon and grieving so hard, somehow her mind had equated Luke with solace. With the happiness she'd known before the tragedy. That's probably why his reaction to seeing her had been such a shock.

The Luke she'd known all her life, the Luke who'd taught her how to climb a tree, the Luke who'd played and *laughed* with her...would never have reacted like that to seeing her.

But, other than catching a rare glimpse of his north end heading south, she hadn't seen Luke Stirling for eight years. Not since he and Brandon left for training at Camp Pendleton. Brandon had come home whenever he could during his years of service. Luke had not.

And then, Afghanistan. All that had happened there.

No wonder he was a different man. Her heart broke all over again, because now, she truly had lost both of them.

She should have realized that a year ago. That when he first came home and didn't come to see her, he didn't *want* to see her. She thought maybe he'd been busy getting things in order after his grandfather's death. And then, she'd heard he'd gone to Seattle to donate bone marrow to his niece, Emma.

But he hadn't just been busy. He'd been avoiding her.

Her stupid heart twanged.

Dang. It really hurt.

She sucked in a deep breath and blew it out slowly. She had no clue what Luke had gone through, what hell he'd faced after the IED. Yes, she'd noticed the scars on his face. The thought of him suffering so horribly made her want to weep. But not as much as that cold emotionless look in his eyes—

"Mom. You're burning it."

Crap. She yanked the pot off the flame. Who burned mac and cheese? "Sorry. Um, go set the table, please."

Her son made a face, but plodded to the breakfront to pull out his place mat and silverware.

Back when she'd been a kid living with her grandmother, that was all it took to make life normal. A set table, and all was well with the world. Why was life so much more complicated now?

"Can I watch TV while I eat?" Jack asked as she ladled this gastronomical delight onto his plate... avoiding the burned bits on the bottom.

She sighed as she sat. "No. I think we need to have a talk."

He groaned. Just like his father, he hated to *talk*.

"Do you want to tell me what happened today? Now that we're home? In private?" she asked as she set his plate before him.

He lifted a shoulder and poked at the macaroni with his fork. "I dunno."

"I need a little more than that. Mrs. Anders may decide to expel you."

He made a face. "So?"

She gave him the eye. "You punched another boy, Jack. That's not okay. And it's not the first time, is it?" When he rolled his eyes, she added, "Just tell me why, hon."

"Fine." He blew out a breath. "He was teasing me and he wouldn't stop and the others were laughing."

"So you punched him?"

"Mmm-hmm."

"You know that's wrong, don't you?"

He nodded. His eyes filled with tears, but sweet manly Jack just wiped them away. "It was the only way to make them stop," he said to his plate.

"I see." She observed him for a moment, wishing so bad Brandon was here with her, and tears pricked her own lashes as well. "Do you want to tell me what they were teasing you about?"

Silently, he shook his head.

"Jack. I really need to know."

"I told you I don't want to talk about it," he bellowed, pushing away from the table.

"Don't use that tone with me, young man. And you have not been excused. Sit back down."

Ah, the rebellion on his face spoke volumes as he stomped back and threw himself into the chair. When he crossed his arms, the action tugged down his T-shirt and she caught a flash of purple on his skin. Her pulse pinged. "What is this?" she asked, reaching over to pull down on his collar. A large mottled bruise covered his shoulder. "Oh, baby. Who did this?"

He pulled away and glared at her. "It's nothing."

"It's not nothing. Did one of those boys hit you, too?"

Again, he shrugged.

God! She hated it when he wouldn't talk to her. Without a word, she went into her workroom and pulled out a balm she'd created using herbs and essential oils for massage clients who were dealing with pain and subdural injuries. She made him sit still as she rubbed it on the ugly bruise, though this was clearly torture for him. And, to be frank, for her. Putting a fragrant ointment on a boy was a little bit like bathing a cat. But she felt better for having done something.

She wished he was small again, so she could pull him into her arms and hug the world away. But he was eight, and eight-year-olds didn't even allow their mothers to kiss them goodbye anymore.

In the end, she gave in and let him watch TV after he finished, but only because she simply didn't have anything left in her tank. Nothing but anger, frustration…and determination to find out what was happening with her son. She had to protect him. She was all he had left.

* * *

Luke sat on his chair, elbows on his knees, fingers laced, staring at nothing. Not even his music could lift this melancholy, so he'd switched it off.

He didn't like this. Didn't like this at all.

Music had always been able to take him away from the world he was trapped in, away from this damaged body. But not anymore.

Thanks to her.

He'd been right to avoid her when he came back to town, because after just one second, just one look into her eyes, his guilt had swamped him.

He let it wash over him because he deserved it. He was the reason she was a widow, the reason Brandon was dead and gone, and there was nothing that could change that.

God. Brandon. How he missed him.

They'd been friends since grade school, he and Brandon. They'd met in the back row during the second grade, where Mr. Pauley put the "dumb" kids. Mr. Pauley didn't actually say that, but everyone else in the class knew what the back row meant. Some reminded him. Frequently.

He and Brandon had been two peas in a pod. They were both terrible at school, but really good at getting what they wanted without following the rules. They both got into trouble and they both got into fights a lot, so yeah, they'd bonded immediately.

They'd been so much alike, Luke thought they

should have been brothers. He was certainly more like Brandon than his real siblings, who were, as far as he could tell, disgustingly perfect in every way.

God knew he tried to shine like DJ, Mark and Sam. But, no matter what, he somehow always failed...in the old man's eyes at least. Each and every time.

His brothers and sister didn't see it. Couldn't understand. Or maybe they pretended to ignore it. But it was clear as day to Luke. He wasn't as good as they were. He sure as hell wasn't as smart. Not book-smart, at least. Too bad that was the only kind of smart that had mattered to the old man.

When it came to the getting-around-whatever-it-was kind of smart, Luke kicked ass. For example, he was smart enough to get the hell out of Butter-scotch Ridge as soon as he could. Smart enough to never look back. And he had thrived in the military. He'd loved the job, the people, the excitement, the fear. All of it. He'd even figured out something very important.

He *wasn't* stupid, as the old man used to holler. Nope. It was something else that made him different—a learning challenge called dyslexia.

Luke refused to call it a learning disability.

Dyslexia was something lots of people had. *Smart* people. And many of them had figured out how to work around it, too.

It had been a life-changing revelation to discover

that he didn't have to live a limited existence. Once Luke discovered audio books and video courses—which made learning much easier than the books he'd struggled with for years—his world opened like a flower. So much flowed in—nourishment for a starving brain that, up until now, had been denied sustenance. He learned about military strategy, classical philosophy, art, music and more. The world was an amazing trove of fascinating information.

He'd shared everything with Brandon, who'd followed him into the service. Brandon, who'd had a form of dyslexia, too. They'd both flourished.

And then, they'd been sent to Afghanistan. Their tour there was exciting and scary and sad. There'd been a lot of drinking, a modicum of learning and amazing bonds that lasted a lifetime. Kind of like college, Luke imagined. And Brandon had been there, by his side, making each and every moment… better. It was like having family there in the desert with him.

And then, one day, Luke went out to work, with Brandon by his side—just like any other day—and woke up three weeks later in a hospital in Germany unable to so much as wiggle his toe.

Once he was cogent, he was told that there had been an explosion, an IED. Shrapnel and debris had blown through the left side of his body, severely damaging the nerves and muscles in his arm and leg. The metal sheet that had cut Brandon's jugular had also slashed Luke's face, leaving a serrated wound. And he was at serious risk of losing the sight in his left eye.

And then came the pause. That horrible pause before they say, "Your spine has been damaged. It is possible that you may never walk again."

But before Luke had time to contemplate that horrific fact, the next hit him.

Brandon was dead.

A band tightened around Luke's head. He clenched his fists so hard his finger bones cracked.

He never should have come, the idiot. He should never have joined up. But he did. Because I did. And now he's dead.

It was too painful to think about, too painful to own. Guilt clawed at his soul, as fresh as the day it began.

Suddenly, his privacy felt like a prison. Suddenly, he felt the need to escape.

It was Friday night, so Crystal would have the night off. It would be safe to go to the bar and get smashed, which was a good thing. Because he really needed to get drunk tonight, if only to silence the guilt.

He wasn't much of a drinker and definitely not a fan of hard liquor, but after the day he'd had—running into Trent, coming face-to-face with Crystal and Brandon's kid—a little oblivion sounded pretty damn good.

* * *

It was a crazy night at the B&G. Felt like there was something in the air, maybe, urging men to madness.

Crystal sighed and adjusted her apron, then grabbed another full tray of drinks for Trent Cooper's table. She dreaded the task. As usual, their weekly poker game had devolved into a bacchanal. The last three times she'd brought them refills, at least one of them had tried to grab her butt. Chase had given her permission to cut them off if they got too rowdy, but she knew if she did, something nasty would break out. Then again, it might anyway. Damn, but she hated working Friday nights. But Chase needed her, and she owed him for letting her skip her afternoon shift to get Jack.

As she approached Trent's table, a chorus of laughter rose. It was the kind of laughter that made a woman's hackles rise. The kind of laughter that made a woman wary. But they barely noticed her, because just as she came close, the front door opened, stealing their leering attention. Someone shouted, "Luke!" and others in the bar echoed his name.

Luke! The sight of him made her pulse flutter. She nearly dropped the tray. Quickly, while the men at the table were goggling over Luke's appearance, she set down the new drinks, cleared the empty glasses and headed back to the bar, trying to still her heart.

She hadn't recovered from their meeting earlier

that day. Couldn't bear to face him again so soon. She did peek, though. Watched him take a seat at the end of the bar. Chase was handling bar orders, so she didn't have to serve Luke, which was a blessing, but as she continued making her rounds, she felt his hot gaze on her.

She probably should have been paying attention to something other than his glare as he knocked back whiskey after whiskey, but she didn't. That was probably why Trent caught her unaware. He grabbed her by the waist as she passed, and yanked her into his lap.

She turned her head to avoid his alcohol-scented halitosis and jabbed him in the chest with her elbow. He released her with a cry of pain—they always did when she gave them the elbow right there—and she sprang away. But he stood and caught her arm before she made her getaway. "That hurt," he snarled. Right into her face. Spittle and all.

God, he was *still* an ass. He'd been an ass ever since kindergarten and had never changed. Using a technique Brandon had taught her on one of his leaves, she jerked her arm out of his hold. "Hands off the merchandise," she said with a smile. It was the kind of move that made most men slink away in fear or humiliation, or whatever emotions bullies actually felt.

It just pissed off Trent.

His face scrunched up and he bristled, his fists

closing as though he intended to hit her. Surreptitiously, she maneuvered her empty tray in position, as a shield, in case he did. She let her expression speak for her.

Back off, buster.

And he did. But only because Chase had been watching, and made his way over and clapped Trent on the shoulder. "Hey, buddy," he said in a calm voice. "Sit down or leave."

"You can't make me leave," Trent snarled.

Chase arched an eyebrow. "Really? There's a sign up front that says we reserve the right to refuse service to anyone. How would you like to be banned from the only watering hole in this town?"

Trent glowered at Crystal, and then took his seat.

Chase nodded. "Good choice." Then he leaned in and whispered, "And keep your hands off the staff." He set a protective hand on Crystal's back, and guided her to the safety of the bar. "You okay?" he asked.

She nodded, tucked an escaped lock behind her ear. "I'm fine. I'm good."

"Wanna switch?" he asked, wondering if she wanted to take over the bar.

She glanced at Luke, who was sitting with his arms on the bar in something like a slump, then glanced at Trent. Yikes. Which was worse? "No. I'm fine. But thanks."

"You sure?" He eyed her worriedly, to which she

brandished her handy-dandy tray. Also, she had no intention of serving that table again. They'd had enough.

"Okey dokey." He sketched a salute and they both went back to work.

After that incident, everything was fine—almost a normal Friday night—until an hour before closing. Then, Trent went to the men's room. When he emerged, he didn't head back to his table. He went straight to Luke. And he stood there, talking to him, talking *at* him, as Luke stared off into the distance.

And then, suddenly, they both glanced at her.

Luke's face went red. Trent smirked.

But when Luke turned away and devoted his attention to his drink once more, Trent's glee dissolved. "Hey. Hey. I'm talking to you," he said in a voice loud enough to carry. "You hear me, Dummy?"

Crystal's gut clenched. Memories flooded her. Memories of Trent and his friends taunting both Brandon and Luke during recess. Saying cruel things. Horrible things. Dummy had been their preferred insult because the bastards had gotten in trouble for using the *R*-word in class.

She shot a warning look at Chase, but he was already watching. Everyone was. Silence fell over the bar like a weighted blanket.

Luke stood with an ominous scrape of his stool. He rose slowly and looked down at Trent's face, only teetering a little. Crystal couldn't hear what he said, but she read his lips, his expression. *Don't call me that.*

Trent smiled. Like a crocodile. A crocodile that had gotten a reaction. "Why not? You always were a dummy. Everyone knows it," he said, giving Luke a hard poke in his left flank.

Luke paled. His gasp was audible. Then his eyes narrowed and he lunged for Trent, who danced out of the way, laughing.

"See? See how *slow* you are?" He turned to his friends, who were watching, stunned and speechless, in something like shock. As though they knew, on some level, that Trent was behaving like a beast, but weren't sure what to do about it. Weren't sure if they should object, or join in.

But Luke knew what to do about it. When Trent leaned in and hissed something that only Luke could hear, his fist came up, and slammed into Trent's face like an anvil; Trent spun around and staggered back.

As satisfying as that was to see, Crystal knew that in the next moment, all hell would break lose, and it did. If there was one thing folks in Butterscotch Ridge loved more than anything, it was a Friday night bar brawl. Crystal had never understood the draw, but in this instance, she had to join in, because most of Trent's friends headed straight for Luke, and that was not a fair fight. Granted, all she had was her tray and some moves Brandon had taught her, but it was oddly satisfying to smack one or two of them on the head, before someone grabbed her arm.

She whirled around…and froze right before bonking her boss.

"What the hell are you doing?" Chase bellowed at her.

"It's not a fair fight!" she bellowed back.

"Really?" They turned just in time to see Luke drop the last of Trent's friends. "He looks like he's doing fine to me."

But then, Luke staggered, sagged to his knees and put a hand to his head, completely helpless, as his combatants started to stir.

"Hell." Chase rushed over and helped Luke to his feet. "Take him upstairs," he barked at her.

Her heart surged. "Upstairs?"

"Quick. I called the police and the last thing he needs, after everything he's been through, is to spend a night in the drunk tank with Trent Cooper."

"Are you sure?" Crystal put her arm around Luke and shouldered his weight. Good God, he was… sturdy.

"Yeah. He didn't start this. Go on. Get him out of here. Hurry. *Before* Cole gets here."

How could she say no? "Come on, buddy," she said to Luke as they stumbled through the kitchen, out the back door and up the stairs to her apartment. She barely made it to the sofa before he collapsed.

He looked up at her with a frown, scrapes and

bruises all over his beautiful face. "You're not supposed to be here," he slurred. Damn, he was drunk.

"I live here," she said, pulling out a throw and easing it over him.

"It's Friday night. You don't work on Friday night. Why did you have to be here?" But, apparently, it was a rhetorical question, because seconds later, his eyes fluttered shut and a snore emanated from his open mouth.

She stared at him for a bit. Gently brushed the shaggy hair from his eyes and stroked his face. Luke was in so much pain. And only some of it was from the fight. With a sigh, she headed to her workroom for the balm that was getting overtime on this particular day. The least she could do was try to relieve some of his pain.

As she spread ointment on his bruised chin, neck and shoulders, she couldn't help thinking how sweet he looked when he was asleep. As though he might just open his eyes at any moment, grin and say, "Hey there, Pickles," the way he used to.

But, of course, he didn't.

Those days were gone.

Chapter Three

Luke woke up with one hell of a headache. It was as though there was a sadistic bongo player in his brain and a Harley idling on his chest. He moved, then groaned, then decided not to move again. It took a little while for him to register a smell. He wasn't sure what it was, but it was pleasant, like wood smoke and eucalyptus.

His brain told him he wasn't outside in the woods, so he cracked open an eye to see if he could solve this mystery. The first thing he saw was a black nose. A face. Whiskers.

Something clicked, and he realized the Harley was a cat, using his chest as a mattress and purring like an engine. He frowned at the thing and it blinked at him, slowly, as though to say, "Yes, I'm using you as my pillow. Whatcha going to do about it?"

Well, hell. He'd always liked cats, anyway. And the rumbling was comforting somehow.

But he didn't have a cat. So…where the hell was he?

The room was not familiar. It was a compact living room/kitchen, decorated in bright colors. There were framed pictures on the wall, clearly crafted by a child, probably with finger paint. A humble abode, for sure, but clean and comfortable.

The mumble of cartoon voices drew his attention to the television.

Though the room was not familiar to him, the boy watching television, cross-legged on the floor, was.

Something bitter rose in his throat.

Damn.

He was in Crystal's apartment.

Double damn.

A vague memory flooded him, along with a mortifying heat. He'd gone to the bar to forget about seeing her again, only to see her again. He'd responded by skulking to the corner of the bar and drinking way too much. He hadn't been that drunk in years, if ever.

He remembered Trent saying really horrible things about Brandon. And Crystal, probably because she'd dodged his drunken attempts to flirt.

His lips curled as he remembered the foggy details of the fight where he beat the crap out of his nemesis of old.

Gently, he tried to move the cat. It settled deeper into his body.

Luke frowned at it. "I need to pee," he said, as though one could convince a cat of anything.

The boy turned his head. "You're awake."

Luke snorted a laugh, which successfully annoyed the cat. It got up, stretched and then sauntered across his body to the top of the sofa and, ultimately, to the windowsill. "I'm alive," he responded. But then, when he tried to sit, he had to doubt that declaration. He felt like hell.

"Bathroom's down the hall." The boy pointed.

"Where's your mom?" Was it wrong that he wanted to just sneak out of here before she woke up?

"She's downstairs at work. She told me to come get her as soon as you woke up."

"You don't need to bother her. I'm leaving." Luke took his time standing, which was a good thing because his head was still fogged up. God, how much had he had to drink last night? The fact that he couldn't remember meant he deserved every ache and pain in his body. He should have turned tail the minute he saw her, rather than trying to drink her away. No one ever successfully drank anything away.

He made his way to the bathroom, using walls

and furniture for balance. The first door he opened wasn't the bathroom, nor was the second. The third was Crystal's bedroom, a pretty, girly room—and empty. He closed the door quickly, fighting down too many contradictory emotions to identify.

They didn't matter. He just had to get out of here before she returned. But when he finished in the bathroom and walked back into the living room, the boy handed him a plate.

"What's this?" he asked gruffly.

"A waffle. I made it for you."

Well, hell. He was a little hungry. "Thanks."

The boy had made one for himself, too, so they sat at the table, across from each other. The boy paused before he started eating, folded his hands and mumbled a prayer over his food, which made Luke feel like a Philistine for just tucking in.

For a toaster waffle, it was pretty good.

A moment of satisfaction, of calm—a carb delirium, perhaps—descended. And then, the boy went and ruined everything.

He looked up at Luke and said, "My mom says you were my dad's friend."

Luke's fork stalled halfway to his mouth. Syrup dripped. "Yeah."

"Can I ask you something?"

Chewing, Luke nodded, his senses alert.

"Were you with him when he died?"

His gut clenched. Damn. He should have expected

this. Luke put down his fork. "I was there." And then, before the kid could throw out any more exquisitely painful questions, Luke asked, "What's that smell?" He twirled his finger in the air. The aroma he'd noticed when he woke up seemed even more pronounced.

Oh. That made the kid laugh. "That's my mom's business."

Luke quirked an eyebrow.

"She makes stinky stuff. People buy it."

"She works at the bar," Luke reminded him.

The boy nodded. A curl flopped onto his forehead. "Not enough money," he said, taking another bite. "She has a couple of jobs."

Luke stilled as a wave of empathy hit him, and he bit back a curse. It wasn't his business what Crystal was going through. He had enough trouble without taking on hers as well. "Does it pay well?"

The kid shrugged. The pajamas slipped down on his skinny shoulders and Luke saw the bruise on his neck. "Whassat?" he asked, waving his fork at the ugly purple mark. He shouldn't have asked. He knew he shouldn't have asked. Didn't know why he did. He should just eat the damn waffle and leave. But no. He had to go and ask.

The kid glanced at Luke from beneath his lids. Then he grinned. "You should see the other guy."

For no reason whatsoever, Luke barked a laugh. He didn't mean to. It just came out. Damn, if the kid wasn't Brandon's Mini-Me. For the first time in a long time, some of Luke's pain eased, but he had no idea why. This was tragic stuff. A fatherless boy. A dead husband. Struggling to survive. Two jobs…

But, for a second there, it had been as though he and Brandon were sharing waffles at this old Formica table. For a second there, there'd been comfort.

"What were you fighting about?" Luke asked. Again, no idea why. Just making conversation, probably.

The boy's expression turned mutinous, then he said, gruffly, "They were talking crap."

Luke nodded. "Been there, done that."

His Brandon-like eyes went wide. "You've been in a fight?"

And, yeah, he had to chuckle again. "Last night, if I remember right."

"Really?"

Whoa. This kid was way too enthusiastic about the subject. "Listen," Luke said. "It's not right to start a fight, but there's nothing wrong with finishing one. You understand what I mean?"

"No."

No? What did he mean *no*? That was pretty sage and clear advice. "What did they say?" he asked instead.

The boy looked away. "Stuff."

"Mmm-hmm. Look, kid. There's stuff and then there's *stuff.*"

Again with the mutinous appearance. "They called me a retard, okay?" This, he hissed. But there was no mistaking the hurt behind his expression.

Luke's gut clenched. *God, he hated that word.* His ire rose, along with his own memories of being called the same. It took a second for him to wrangle those emotions. The last thing Jack needed was his anger piled on top of his own. But damn, it pissed him off, people saying that. "Let me guess. The kids who said that are jerks."

Jack blinked and then his smile quirked. "Yeah."

"Yeah. There were jerks like that around when your dad and I were growing up, too. You can't believe anything they say, you understand? You make your own road."

"Okay." Jack toyed with his fork for a minute and, staring at his waffle, murmured, "They said my dad was, too. You know. Stupid." He shrugged.

It took a long breath in through flared nostrils for Luke to calm himself down. Small towns sucked sometimes. The past followed you forever. You were not allowed to evolve. Not ever.

Jack glanced at him with a pleading expression. "Was he? Was my dad a dummy?"

It took a minute for Luke to swallow his rage and respond. "Listen here. Your dad was one of the smartest men I ever knew. Sure, he wasn't good at reading and math, but he had other smarts, and so do you. Do you hear me?"

The boy didn't answer, just stared at him, and Luke realized he probably sounded like a ranting loon. He sucked in another deep breath, blew it out slowly and calmed himself. "Kid, your dad was what they call dyslexic. I am, too. Yeah, we were terrible at school. Yeah, kids made fun of us. And yeah, it was hard sometimes, I'm not gonna lie. But it gets better. You keep working until you figure things out. You find ways that help you cope."

Mini-Me's eyebrows rumpled. He looked so much like Brandon, Luke almost couldn't breathe for a second there. "Would you help me figure it out?" he asked.

Luke stared at the boy; his entire body shrank into a tight emotional wad. Panic snarled through his gut. Why did the kid's expression have to be so beseeching? His face so much like Brandon's?

Yeah. He was in hell. Had to be.

He needed to get out of here. Now. So he glanced at his watch and stood in a rush. "Sorry, kid, I gotta go. Tell your mom thanks," he said as he bolted from the apartment, like the coward that he was.

Because now he hadn't just failed his best friend—he'd failed Brandon's kid, too.

Crystal pushed through the back door of the B&G just in time to see Luke making his way down the stairs from her apartment. Her chest tightened at the sight of him, and not just because each step seemed to be a challenge for him.

It was ridiculous of her to even notice how handsome he was. Or the bunching muscles in his forearms, or the cut of his slim hips, or the light of concentration on his handsome face. Oh, sure, he had scars, but he was *Luke*. Besides, somehow those scars made him even more attractive.

But then, when he saw her, he froze. His expression changed, tightened. A muscle in his cheek flexed as though he was gritting his teeth. She knew that look. It was his stubborn look. She'd seen it before.

That made her sad. She wasn't an obstacle he needed to push out of the way. Was she?

"Hey," she said in as bright and cheery a tone as she could manage. "I'm glad I caught you. How are you feeling?"

His chin came out. "I'm fine," he said, and then, as though to prove it, he attempted to bound down the remaining stairs. It was a mistake. She could tell right away when he winced and his knees buckled. She pretended to ignore his pain, the white knuckles as he clutched the banister, because she knew him. He hated when people pitied him.

So there was not a lick of compassion in her tone as she brightly chirped, "Good to hear." Before he could turn to leave—which he clearly intended to do—she added, "There's something I'd like to talk to you about."

His nostrils flared. "Right now?"

"It'll only take a minute." And then, because he was leaning into a turn, she said quickly, "Luke. I... need your help."

He reared back and stared at her. "*My* help?"

Oh, for pity's sake. She wasn't asking for a kidney. "Did you, ah, get a chance to meet my son, Jack?"

His brow furrowed as though he didn't care for where this was going. "In passing."

"He's so much like Brandon. Did you notice?" His frown darkened. Since he didn't answer, she plowed on. "He's strong, like his dad. Independent. Maybe a little rebellious..."

He raked back his hair. "Look, Crystal. I'm late. I have to get to the ranch—"

"Please. Can you give me five minutes?" Five minutes for the friendship they'd once had. That wasn't too much to ask for, was it?

He glanced at his watch. "All right. But I really have to go."

"Can we go inside and sit down?" She waved at the back door of the B&G. "I'll buy you breakfast."

"I've already eaten." His mouth lifted in a slight smile. "Jack gave me a waffle."

Damn. He was working really hard to not spend time with her, wasn't he? She had no idea why, but it broke her heart to see this stranger in Luke's body. For a nanosecond she thought about just letting him go, but she was stubborn, too. She'd do anything to protect her son.

Just like a mama bear.

She crossed her arms and glared at him. Didn't say anything, just glared until he became uncomfortable and shifted his feet. It was a skill she'd learned in the last eight years, raising a son practically on her own.

When he shoved his hands into the pockets of his jeans, she figured she'd chastened him enough. She softened her expression and her tone. "With Brandon… gone, Jack really needs a male role model. Someone who can, you know, show him the ropes of growing up. I was thinking that it might be good for—"

He cut her off with a barked laugh. "And you thought of me?"

Yes. Yes, of course. "Luke, Jack is your best friend's son."

If anything, his face became stonier, which made her stomach curdle. That bleak expression was back, the one she didn't really understand. It sent chills through her.

"Luke—"

"No." He shook his head and turned to walk away. But before he did, he glanced back at her and, in a despondent tone, said, "I'm the last man you want around your son, Crystal."

"You're wrong."

"I wish I was," he said. "Look at me. I'm all broken myself. How the hell can you expect me to fix things for you when I can't fix my own life? No." And, when she opened her mouth to try to convince him to reconsider, he repeated himself. "No, Crystal. I'm sorry. You need to find someone else. I'm not the one."

She watched him walk away until he turned the corner, her soul swamped with sadness and loss. Hardly a new feeling for her in the last three years. But this was fresh grief. Fresh grief for Luke. Because this was undeniable confirmation that the boy she'd known and loved was lost.

Things didn't get any better for Crystal the following week. Tuesday was particularly frustrating. It had started off with an overflowing toilet and the cat vomiting hair balls all over the carpet. Jack had moved so slowly getting ready for school—changing his T-shirt several times—that she was almost late for work. Then Tiffany, the waitress she was trying to train, had dropped a full tray of meals when she went through the wrong door into the dining room, even though the In and Out doors were clearly marked.

Tiffany ran out the back crying, leaving Crystal to not only clean up the mess, but also cover her tables.

Sometimes, doing it yourself was definitely easier than training someone. Too bad she didn't have a clone.

Thankfully, once the lunch rush was over, Crystal had a little time to relax. And by relax, she meant wiping down tables. It was mindless work so sometimes she enjoyed it.

Her reprieve was cut short when Chase called her over to the bar.

"What?" she asked with uncustomary abruptness.

"Whoa. Somebody's in a bad mood."

Crystal shook her head and blew out a sigh. "Sorry. It's been a rough day. What do you need?"

He grimaced. "Um, you got a phone call." He handed her the receiver of the ancient rotary phone with a sympathetic glance. *Damn it.* There was only one reason Crystal ever received calls at her work number, and they both knew what it was. "It's Stella Anders."

Of course, it was.

With tightening fingers and a roiling gut, Crystal listened silently to an outraged monologue from the principal. She didn't even have the energy to mumble her usual apologies.

Jack had been in another fight. The other boy had been rushed to the clinic and needed five stitches. The parents were considering getting a restraining order against her baby. Oh, and by the way, Jack was suspended. Stella recommended counseling to help deal with his frustration and anger.

Counseling? Crystal simply didn't have the money for a therapist or a counselor. It certainly wasn't covered in the scanty health insurance Chase could afford to give her. She'd probably have to look at a larger town—like Spokane, over two hours away—to find a specialist.

After Stella hung up, Crystal clung to the phone with numb fingers. Dread, anger and frustration swirled through her. She had no idea what was eating away at her son, and no idea what to do about it.

Good God. She was tired. So tired. All she wanted was to go upstairs and take a nap. But she couldn't. She had to go, pick up her scoundrel of a son, then come back here to knock out a double shift, and then somehow, miraculously—in the middle of the night, perhaps—finish an essential-oil order that was due to be shipped tomorrow.

This wasn't how life was supposed to be. Was it? Oh, it was exhausting. Utterly exhausting. Too much. It was so much easier to pretend it wasn't happening. Or quit. Run away.

But mothers didn't do that. Mothers stiffened their spines and got creative and figured something out.

She was all Jack had now. And she would find a way to make it work. For his sake.

But, damn, it was hard to do everything all alone.

Luke shifted on his saddle and tipped back his Stetson so he could glance over his shoulder at his brother Danny, who was behind him, rounding up the stragglers as they moved the herd for the winter. It was just October, but forecasters were predicting a cold snap so it made sense to move them now. When the snow fell out here on the range, it fell hard. It wasn't unheard of to get six feet overnight. Ranchers who'd been caught out had lost entire herds.

Unfortunately, because this wasn't work that required a lot of concentration, his mind had been wandering.

And Luke didn't like where it went.

In short, his conscience was eating at him and had been since his visit to Crystal's place. That boy— Brandon's son—kept popping into his mind with annoying regularity. Thank God Luke had plenty of good old-fashioned work to distract him.

He wasn't as limber as his brothers, but he could get things done. Granted, most things took him longer, but he could still *do* things—for which he was grateful. Hell, he didn't know who he'd be if he couldn't ride a horse.

"Hey. Need any help?" he called to his brother.

Danny shot him a grin. "I got 'em," he hollered back. Then he whipped his horse around and cut off an obstinate heifer, guiding her back to the others.

It was pretty amazing to watch. Not because Luke hadn't seen someone herd cattle before. He had. It was that Danny was so dang good at it. It was hard to believe that last year, when he'd arrived in Butterscotch Ridge for the reading of their grandfather's will, Danny had been a stone-cold city slicker who fell out of the saddle more often than he didn't.

Because of the terms of the old man's will, the five heirs were required to work the ranch for a period of three years before anyone could inherit. If one of them defaulted, they all lost out. The entire ranch would go to someone else.

The others didn't realize it, but the old man had put in that codicil specifically for him, to force him to stay in Butterscotch Ridge. The old man had always been an ass.

Luke hadn't thought much of his surprise sibling back then, but that had changed. Danny, previously a Vegas denizen, had thrown himself into not just the ranch work, but into the family, too. Funny, wasn't it? Now it was impossible to think of life without Danny, his wife, Lizzie, and their daughter, Emma.

His lips quirked as he thought of Emma. He adored his niece, and had since the day they'd met.

He'd certainly never imagined he would fall in love with the little girl, who'd once been so sick a cold could kill her. In fact, when Danny told them about his daughter—who needed a bone-marrow transplant to fight off a rare disease—Luke hadn't really *grasped* what that meant. When they all decided to go to Seattle to meet this little girl, and be tested to see if they were a match—because they were, apparently, blood relatives—he'd just gone along, even though he hated hospitals with a passion.

Of course, Emma's hospital had been different from the institutional military hospitals he'd experienced after his injury. Her hospital was painted in cheerful colors and staffed by nurses wearing Winnie the Pooh scrubs.

But even with all of that, Luke hadn't really understood the weight of it, the impact of it, until Emma had crawled into his lap and asked to touch his scars.

And then...

And then, she'd smiled at him. Smiled and said, "It feels just like my scars."

You're not so different from me.

We're alike.

We'll take care of each other.

Yeah. She hadn't said those words but he'd heard them in his heart. And that heart would never be the same again.

When word came back that he was the perfect donor, he was the one who could save sweet Emma, Luke had felt a surge of power. He wasn't the same kid who left Butterscotch Ridge with a chip on his shoulder. He was a strong man. A man who didn't give up. He was a man who helped others when he could. Saving Emma had been the best feeling he'd known since Brandon died.

An irritating thought, one he'd been ignoring for days now, niggled its way into his brain and a pang of guilt stabbed at him. If he was being honest, it had been stabbing him since he left Crystal's apartment on Saturday.

Since he left Jack.

Was he a man who helped others when he could? Was he, really? Because there was Jack, his best friend's son, a kid with a learning disability, just like he'd once been. The boy had pleaded with him for answers, for God's sake. And what had he done? Fled.

And why?

Because he'd been afraid. Afraid of the pain such interactions might cause.

Yeah. It was true. It was painful looking into Jack's face. Or Crystal's for that matter. It made him think of Brandon, which caused that swelling of emptiness and anger and guilt.

And which was worse, really? The pain of his memory, or the shame of letting him down? Again?

Luke pulled off his Stetson to wipe his brow. Though the day had an autumn briskness, the sun was still hot on his head. That was a mere irritation compared with the heat of shame strafing him.

In his life, he'd known pain beyond bearing, but here he was, just causing more pain for others in a pathetic attempt to avoid hurting himself. How selfish was that?

Was that the kind of man he wanted to be? Was that the kind of man he was?

By the time they reached lower pasture, he'd realized he had to help that boy.

Even if it meant seeing Crystal again. Even if it meant facing his grief and guilt again. Even if it meant smelling her scent again.

He had to help that boy.

It was the right thing to do.

It was what Brandon would have wanted.

The last thing Crystal expected on Wednesday morning—her first day off in three weeks—was a knock on her door before she'd even had a moment to pour herself a cup of coffee.

No. Strike that.

The last thing she expected was to open the door to find Luke Stirling standing at the top of the stairs. Her heart gave an annoying jump. A familiar jump, but annoying all the same. She hadn't seen hide nor hair of him since that night he'd taken drunken refuge in her home.

She and Luke had known each other since kindergarten. They'd been *friends* since kindergarten. Still, despite all this, Crystal couldn't, for the life of her, come up with anything to say. After a long and pregnant pause, she choked out, "Luke."

He nodded, his expression somber. "Crystal. Do you have some time? We need to talk."

Oh, crap. With effort, she forced a smile. "Sure.

Come in." She stepped back so he could pass, then closed the door quietly.

"Is Jack here?" he asked after a quick glance around the room.

"He's sleeping."

Luke arched an eyebrow. "Not at school?"

She held back her sigh, forced a smile and shook her head. "Not today." Not for the next week, according to Stella Anders. If Luke had a real relationship with anyone but himself, he would have heard about that through the grapevine. "Can I get you a cup of coffee?"

The tight lines around his lips relaxed, just a little. "That would be great. Yeah."

"Go ahead and have a seat," she said, waving at the table on her way to the coffeepot. By the time she poured two mugs and filled a plate with muffins, he was settled in.

She had to take a moment longer, though, to prepare herself to face him. His scent—something earthy, something purely masculine—filled her nostrils, as his presence filled the room. Drawing a deep, calming breath, she turned and...nearly dropped the coffee.

Good lord, he was so attractive—large and lanky with broad shoulders and narrow hips. His powerful body was packed into well-worn jeans and a humble work shirt. His hair, slightly too long, tumbled onto his forehead, framing his slate-gray eyes. As for his face—it was classical perfection. Even his scars could not ruin that perfection. Perhaps they enhanced it.

It was a sin that he was heartbreakingly beautiful on the outside and so cold on the inside.

She must have paused too long, because his brow furrowed. "Do you need some help?"

"No. Not at all. Here." She set his mug in front of him, and hers at her place, then quickly fetched the plate from the counter. "Something to eat. If you're hungry." And then she cringed, because, *duh*. He probably knew muffins were food. "Oh. Milk or sugar?"

And to this, he shook his head. They sat in silence as they sipped for a moment. When that moment became too uncomfortable for her, she had to speak. "You wanted to talk?"

"Yeah." He stared into his cup. A flush rose on his cheeks. He paused so long she had to wonder if he intended to continue. Finally, he looked up, caught her gaze and said, "I'm sorry I left like that the other day."

Well, as apologies went, it wasn't bad. Not enough, but not bad."

"Okay."

He gored her with those steely gray eyes. "No. It's not okay. For one thing, I left without thanking you. So I wanted to say thank you, too."

"You don't need to thank me. We're friends, Luke.

And friends take care of each other." Without thinking she reached out and set her hand on his. She didn't expect him to jerk away.

She didn't think that tiny rejection should hurt as much as it did.

"Are we friends?" he asked in a hollow voice.

She swallowed heavily at the pain in his gaze. She couldn't quite interpret it, but didn't need to. "We've always been friends. Since we were kids." The Three Musketeers. "Nothing can change that."

"Nothing?"

"Nothing, Luke," she said with undue harshness. Or maybe he needed the harshness—maybe he needed her adamant tone, to believe her—because she saw it there, in his eyes, when he accepted it. Accepted the fact that even though Brandon was gone, *they* could still be friends. This time, when she took his hand, he let her. He even curled his fingers around hers and gave a little squeeze.

"But that's not the only reason I came by. I want to help your son," he said baldly. "I really think I can."

Chapter Four

The hairpin turn of the conversation threw her. "What do you mean?"

He released her hand and leaned back in his chair. "That morning, before you and I talked, Jack and I…had a chat."

"Really?" She tried not to feel hurt that Jack hadn't mentioned it. "What did you talk about?"

"The trouble he's having at school, mostly. He's having the same problems Brandon and I had, you know."

She nodded even though she hadn't known. Not really. Of course, she knew that Luke and Brandon had often gotten into trouble—but it wasn't something Brandon had ever talked about.

"Well, like I said, I think I can help him."

Crystal stared at Luke, her mind spinning. "Wait. Help him with what? He won't even tell me what's wrong." Sometimes it sucked, being a mother. When your child needed something and wouldn't turn to you if you were the last person on the planet.

To her surprise, Luke grinned. It was the first time she'd seen that light dancing in his eyes since… well, before, so it stunned her a little. She'd forgotten how utterly dazzling that smile was. It almost made her let down her defenses, but she knew better.

"I get why he doesn't want to talk to you," he said with a chuckle. Her awe at his physical beauty quickly turned to irritation.

"What's so funny?"

"Oh." He sobered, but she was pretty sure it was just to placate her. "Sorry. It's not that it's funny, it's just… You're the mom."

"I know I'm the mom." A bit of a snap.

"Sometimes it's hard to confess difficult things to a female, especially your *mom*. It's easier to talk man-to-man."

"Oh." Honestly, what could she say to that?

"You remember me when I was eight?"

She nodded, even though it had been a long time ago, and when you've known someone your entire life, it's difficult to pinpoint something as specific as "eight."

"I was in a fight every other day. Remember?"

Oh, yes. She remembered that. Both he and Brandon had been hellions.

"So you're saying it's normal?" It didn't feel normal. Other boys didn't get suspended from school on a regular basis.

Luke raked back his hair, revealing a spider web of scars on his forehead. "Hell, I don't even know what normal is. But I'll tell you this, I know why Jack is fighting."

"Because his father died?"

"Well, maybe a little bit of that. I don't know. But I think the real problem stems from his learning challenges."

She frowned at him. "He's in a special program that's supposed to be helping him with reading and math. Are you saying that's why he gets in trouble?"

"No." Luke went all somber again. "He gets in trouble because he's frustrated. The kind of teaching methods that work for other kids don't work for him. He can never succeed because their paradigm of success doesn't apply to us."

Something pinged in the general region of her chest. *"Us?"*

Luke nodded sheepishly. "I'm dyslexic, too. So was Brandon. You remember how we both struggled in school?"

"Sure." She'd never understood it because Luke and Brandon were both so smart. Everyone had just assumed they didn't give a damn about school. And she had, too, which filled her with shame…and a good portion of terror for her son. "So Jack gets into fights because he feels like a failure?"

"I know I did, most of my life." Her chest tightened as she imagined little-boy Luke thinking he was a failure. That was just so…wrong. "But there's more," he continued. "Jack fights because the other boys are bullying him."

The air whooshed out of her lungs. Her heart thudded. A little muscle in her eye twanged. "They're bullying him?" Fury rose up within her, burning away all other emotions, including her irritation with Luke. "So every time Jack has been in a fight, every time I've been called in and hauled before a teacher or the principal…someone else started it? By tormenting my boy?" Damn it. He was grinning again. "What?" she barked. "What's so funny?"

"Nothing," he said. "I just wish I'd had someone like you to storm in and defend me. That's all. You really are a great mom."

She wasn't ready to release her ire, not even in the face of his very perceptive observation. "I can't believe those kids have been picking on my baby and he didn't tell me."

"Yeah. Maybe don't call him your baby anymore." And, when she glowered at him, he grinned. "He's eight, after all. Practically a man."

All right. She did smile at that. But only a little. She was still miffed at him for being a jerk, but this conversation had gone a long way toward making up for that. The fact that he'd made the effort—that he'd admitted he'd been wrong and wanted to help fix things—showed the true character of the man he'd become. "Okay. Now I have a better handle of what's going on, and I really appreciate that. Thank you, Luke."

He glanced at the bottom of his empty mug. "I was thinking maybe, if you don't mind, I could tutor Jack. You know, show him some of the skills I've used to deal with dyslexia."

This was the last thing she expected to come out of his mouth, but while she was thrilled to the bones that he wanted to help Jack, the terse conversation they'd had the other day made her leery. What if he treated Jack like that? Maybe—

"I can see you don't like the idea. It's okay. I understand. I—"

"I like the idea, Luke. What worries me is…well, you're not the Luke I used to know. The way you treated me on Saturday… I won't expose Jack to that. I just can't."

He closed his eyes. The muscle on his cheek flexed. A red tide rose on his face. The silence crackled around them. "I… You deserved so much better from me, Crystal. I know it. I don't have any excuse."

All right. "Do you have a reason?"

It took him a minute to formulate his response. "I... You both remind me of Brandon. So much." He looked at her then. Swallowed heavily. "It was too painful for me to... It still is. But I realized by trying to avoid that pain for myself, I was causing more pain for you and Jack and that was wrong." He took her hand, gently, like it was delicate porcelain. "I am so, so sorry, Crystal. I hope you can look past that. I hope you can forgive me..."

Her heart swelled. Oh, heavens. Maybe there was a bit of the old Luke in there somewhere after all.

His brow furrowed. "What's wrong?"

"What? Nothing."

"Why are you crying?"

Was she? Oh, dear. Perhaps she was. She reached for a napkin and blew her nose loudly. "I'm just glad you're here, Luke. I'm glad we're...friends again." She couldn't go back to the way it was before. And she wouldn't let him. "And I'm so happy you want to help Jack."

"So...you're okay with my idea?"

"Yes," she said, almost before he was done talking. "Yes. Please." Oh, the relief and gratitude filling her soul was so delicious. The mystery that had been tormenting her was solved. And Luke was here. Luke was going to help. She wasn't all alone in this anymore!

"I'll want to talk to him first. You know. See if he's interested," he said.

She leaned in. "He'll be interested."

Luke barked a laugh. "It's important that he makes the decision. It's his future. His life. He already asked me for help and…"

"And what?"

He scrubbed his face with a broad hand. "I'm ashamed to say, I walked away. But to be honest, I wasn't ready then. I am ready now. It's my obligation."

Crystal frowned. "I don't like that idea. You feeling *obligated*."

"You don't understand. It's not that I feel motivated by guilt—it's not that kind of obligation. It's something deeper. Like a spiritual obligation. Someone helped me. I feel the need to pay it forward."

The intensity of his response caught her a little off guard. "Who helped you, Luke?" she asked softly.

He lifted a shoulder. "A lot of people actually. The first was my drill sergeant at Pendleton. He noticed I had transposed some numbers on a report, and he asked me if I'd ever been tested for dyslexia. Of course, I had no idea what it was. He got me some special training and pointed me to some really great resources. I found out later that his daughter was dealing with it, too."

"That was a lucky break."

"Mmm-hmm. And then there was this one nurse

at Walter Reed." He spoke with such admiration, it made Crystal feel a prick of jealousy, even though she had no claim on Luke, or his affection, at all.

"What did she teach you?" she asked.

Her question caught his attention and he snorted a laugh. "He."

"Oh." She had no idea why that pang of jealousy stabbed at her, but there it was again.

"Lieutenant Duncan introduced me to video learning. I didn't have anything to do when I wasn't in physical therapy…" He broke off for a moment. "Anyway, I spent that time learning all sorts of things."

She had to ask. "Such as?"

"Well, let's just say if you're interested in the eruption of Mount Vesuvius in 70 AD, I'm your guy."

"Ancient history, eh?"

"Love it. Fall of Rome too…"

"Et tu, Brute?" Crystal leaned back in her chair, unable to stop grinning. Yes. Yes. *This* was what she remembered, this was what she'd missed so much. Just talking and laughing with nothing between them, not even the ghost of her dead husband. Perhaps, especially not that.

"More coffee?" she asked as she stood to refill her own cup.

She was pleased when he said yes. That meant

he wasn't in a hurry to leave. That meant this lovely moment could continue.

"Of course," she said as she sat the fresh cups on the table, "if you're spending your valuable time helping Jack, you'll have to let me repay you."

The suddenness of his withdrawal shocked her. "No," he said as a cold mask descended.

"Luke…"

"I said no."

Good God, he was being stubborn. Why should she be surprised? He'd always been mulish. "I don't want to take advantage of your generosity—"

"Come on, Crystal," he snapped. "You're a single mother with two jobs."

She frowned. "Technically, three."

"Three? Really?" He blew out a breath and raked his hair.

She put back her shoulders and tipped up her chin. "Lots of women hold down multiple jobs these days."

"I'm aware. Point is, I'm not taking your money for helping Jack."

"Well, maybe I wasn't even thinking about money. What about that?"

His eyes narrowed on her, skimmed over her breasts, lingered on her lips. "What are you suggesting?" he asked, his voice oddly choked.

Her frown deepened. *Not that!* "I noticed you were limping when you came in. I mean, more than usual." He frowned at her, but she barreled on before he could stop her. "I have a license in massage therapy with some course work in craniosacral practices. I thought maybe I could help you with the pain."

He gaped. "You have a license in massage therapy?"

"Yes." Why was he so surprised? "It was my plan to open a storefront..." She trailed off before she mentioned that Brandon's death had killed her dreams as well. "Well, anyway. I'm very good at what I do. I'm happy to trade tutoring for massages."

He shook his head. "I don't think so."

"I *know* I can help you."

For some reason, he flinched. "That's not necessary."

"Necessary, schmeshessary. We're friends. We help each other. That's what we do." She pushed on, because he was getting that truculent look on his face again. "I could really help ease your pain, at least a little, Luke. I know I could."

"I'm sure you are wonderful," he said, again looking into his cup. "The fact is, I had my share of massage therapy when I was at Walter Reed and the VA. It's... It's too painful. I..." He sighed, and then he continued, almost in a whisper, "I can't stand being touched. It's too..."

She set her hand on his again, if only to stop this tortured admission. "All right. I get it. I understand. But let me at least give you a balm I made.

It's got some natural pain relievers in it. Maybe that will help."

He made a credible attempt at a smile and nodded. "Okay. That would be fine."

"And maybe I can throw in a home-cooked meal once in a while?"

"All right," he assented, but gruffly.

"Good." She knew, deep down, that it was huge for him to accept anything—from anyone—and she was grateful to be able to help him, in any way that he'd allow. "But if you ever change your mind… If you ever decide you want to try these magic hands…" She waggled her fingers for humorous effect, and it worked. He chuckled.

"You'll be the one I'll call."

"Promise?"

"I promise."

"Good."

She hoped he did take her up on it, and not just because she owed him for shedding light on the mystery of Jack's behavior and offering to tutor him. But because she sensed a deep pain within him, one that she ached to soothe. In any way she could.

It was the least she could do for the man who was so willing to help her son.

For some reason Luke was nervous when he sat down with Jack; maybe he was worried the boy would reject his help…which Luke would probably deserve at this point. Or maybe Luke was worried Jack would accept it. The boy's expression was certainly sullen when he emerged from his bedroom and saw Luke sitting at the kitchen table.

"Good morning, sweetheart," Crystal said, getting up to kiss him on the forehead. "Are you hungry?"

The boy frowned at them both in turn, and then shrugged.

Luke cleared his throat. "I'm heading down to the B&G. Want to join me for breakfast? I thought we could have a talk. You know. Man-to-man." Jack's eyes narrowed, as though he was trying to suss out Luke's sincerity. So he added, "I'd like to continue that conversation we had the last time I was here. If you don't mind."

A slender shoulder shrugged. "Whatever."

"Great." Luke stood and pushed in his chair. "Thanks for the coffee, Crystal. Jack and I won't be too long. I promise."

She nodded. "All right. I'll be right here if you need me." This last bit was directed to her son, who grunted in response. But he did follow Luke out the door and down the stairs.

Once they stepped inside the B&G, Luke opted for a booth away from the other customers. He glanced at Jack. "Is this okay?"

Another shrug, but this one was accompanied by a sullen "Sure."

Though Luke wanted to launch right into his proposal, he decided it might be better to wait until they had their food before tackling the business at hand. The boy didn't seem overly anxious to start there, either. He surveyed the menu in silence.

"Anything look good?" he asked, by way of small talk.

Jack lowered the menu and sent him a challenging look. "A chocolate milkshake."

"For breakfast?" Would Crystal be okay with that? Then, he thought better of taking a parental tack. After all, he wanted to try and convince Jack to let him help...maybe a little ice cream for breakfast wasn't the end of the world. "Uh, okay."

"With whipped cream on top."

"Is there any other kind?"

The kid's eyes narrowed again. "So you're going to let me have a milkshake? For breakfast?"

Luke shrugged. "Why not?"

"My mom wouldn't approve."

"I reckon my mom wouldn't have, either. But it's your decision." He knew, instinctively, that Jack was testing him, but the bald fact was, a chocolate milkshake sounded pretty good. For some reason, his failure to rise to the bait made Jack even more sullen.

When the waitress came by—a young girl named Tiffany who'd spilled an entire soda pop in Luke's lap the last time he was here—he girded his loins.

"Coffee?" she asked, waving a half-full pot at him. *Egads.*

"No. No thanks," he said. "I'll have water." At least water didn't hurt when poured on a man's crotch. "You ready to order?" he asked Jack.

The boy nodded. "I'll have waffles." He shot a glance at Luke. "With whipped cream."

"Great," Tiffany said between chomps on her gum as she scribbled the order on a pad. "And you, sir?"

"I'll have the farmhouse breakfast with eggs over easy, cottage fries crisp and well-done bacon."

Jack's eyes widened. "Oh, I want bacon, too."

"Well done or floppy?" Tiffany asked.

The boy glanced at Luke again, straightened his spine and said, "Well done."

Luke nodded in approval. No one liked limp bacon. He had no idea why people even bothered to make it like that. Might as well just suck on it raw. "How about that milkshake?"

Jack dropped his menu on the table. "Maybe some other time."

"Okay." Luke pretended to be uninterested in the choice, but the truth was, he was pleased that the boy had made a good decision on his own. It boded well for what he had in mind. As soon as they were alone, he leaned in and said quietly, "So you remember when you asked me to help you—"

Jack leaned back and crossed his arms. "And you walked away?"

Ouch. That stung. And he had to admit, he deserved it. "Yeah. That. Okay. I was a jerk. I'm sorry."

"Fine. Is that all you wanted to say?"

"No. I've thought it over, and I would like to help you, if it's something you still want to do."

The boy surveyed him with a contemplative look. Then he nodded. "I suppose."

"It's totally up to you, but what I want you to know is I understand how you feel."

A scoff. "Right."

"I do. The bullies, the teachers, the tests. All of it. I've been through it all."

"And why do you want to help me?"

Luke thought about that for a moment, just so he could find the right words. "I guess, because I went through it, and I know how crappy it was—" Jack's eyes widened at his curse word. "I wish someone had been there to help me, you know, when I was a kid and it mattered. I wish someone had been there to explain to me and your dad that we weren't stupid. That our brains just…work differently. Mostly, I wish there had been someone there to teach me how to, I don't know, play their game. Do you understand?"

Jack shook his head. A curl, just like Brandon's, flopped on his forehead, causing Luke's chest to tighten. "How's that gonna help me learn better?"

"Well..." Luke huffed a laugh. "You're a smart kid. There's ways to learn outside the usual channels, like books. And sometimes the trouble isn't learning, it's showing that you learned. You know how you get an assignment, and they give you a test to see how well you know the material?"

Jack blew out a wet raspberry. "I hate those tests."

"Yeah." Luke chuckled. "I did, too. But what if there was a different way to learn the material, and a different way to show what you learned?"

"What do you mean?"

Luke waited until Tiffany set their plates on the table before he continued, just in case anything went flying. Once she left, and Jack said his little prayer over the food, Luke dug in to his eggs, mashing them up with the potatoes, the way he liked it. "Most learning when I was a kid consisted of reading books."

Jack's nose curled. "I hate books."

"Yeah. I did, too. I had so much trouble reading because the letters—"

"They move."

"Right. And *p*'s and *q*'s—"

"And *b*'s and *d*'s—"

"And the *s*'s that looks like eights—"

Jack chuckled. "I hate that."

Luke nodded. "Me, too. So I found other ways to learn what they wanted me to know, without having to read. There are so many resources out there now,

Jack. There's no reason for you to have to struggle so hard to fit in a square hole."

The button nose wrinkled again. "What does that mean?"

"You're trying to be something you're not—"

"I feel like that."

"When what you are is awesome, just the way you are. You are a great kid, and I bet you've got lots of talents and skills. But dyslexia isn't something that's going to go away, so learning how to live with it, to work with it, is going to serve you all your life."

Jack swallowed and leaned in. "Is it hard? To do what you do?"

Luke leaned closer, too. "Don't tell anyone this, okay?"

"Okay." They spoke in whispers.

"I think of it as a game. When I hit any kind of difficulty, I look for different ways to overcome it. It's like a puzzle to solve. And it can be fun. If you let it."

And Luke saw it, saw that light ignite in Jack's eyes, the light that shines when another person truly sees you. It was one of the most gratifying moments of his life. "I'd like to teach you some of the tricks I learned."

"Like what?"

"Well, for example, instead of a written test, maybe the teacher can sit down and talk to you about what you've learned. Like in history, or social studies."

"And what about math?" He said the last word like it tasted bad.

"I gotta be honest, I still struggle a little with math—the numbers don't fall into patterns the way words do, you know." Jack nodded. "But we can focus on mathematical concepts and ideas. That's what I did when I was learning to fly. You have to understand how numbers relate to each other when you're in the air. Your life depends on it."

"You fly? Like a plane?" His eyes were wide, his mouth agape.

"Mmm-hmm." Luke chomped on his bacon and Jack followed suit. "I gotta tell you, when you really want to learn something, it's easier to break through that wall. Do you know what I mean?"

Jack nodded. "I know the wall. I mean, I feel it when they try to teach me stupid stuff. But…"

"You've never broken past it?"

"Not really."

"I know. I didn't, either, until I started looking at it from a different angle. That's the thing about us. We see the world differently than other people. In fact, there have been a lot of geniuses and inventors who are dyslexic—like Thomas Edison. Because he saw things that other people didn't see. And look what he did—he invented the light bulb."

Jack looked hopeful. "So I'm not…dumb?"

Luke grinned and blew out a breath. "No, kiddo. You are not any of those names *they* called you. You just don't fit in *their* little box. It's time to stop trying that, and try something that does work. Okay?"

"Who else?"

"Huh?"

"Who else is dyslexic?"

Luke shrugged. "A lot of people from history. Woodrow Wilson…"

"Who's that?"

"He was the twenty-eighth president of the United States. Have you heard about Leonardo da Vinci? Stephen Hawking?"

"He was a genius."

"And so many more. Like Hans Christian Andersen."

"Who'sat?" Jack said around a mouthful of waffle.

"He wrote books of fairy tales."

"Books? He wrote books?"

"Yeah."

Jack sat back and glowered at Luke. "How can someone who can't read, write books?"

Luke blew out a breath. "No one can define what you can do. Only you. Anyway, my point is, being different isn't always a bad thing. Who knows what you can accomplish in your lifetime? With the technology we have, it's even easier than when I was a kid. So…" He paused to make sure Jack was paying attention. "I'd really like to show you some of the tricks that have worked for me, if you want to learn. It's totally up to you."

Jack grunted and thought about it for a minute. "What does my mom say?"

"Dude. She loves you. She wants what's best for you. She wants you to be happy, you know."

He sighed. "I know I'm a pain to her—"

"We all are, when we're eight, I think."

"But it's especially hard for her, you know, because Dad…" He leaned closer and said, "She still cries sometimes at night."

Luke's chest tightened. He cleared his throat. "Yeah. I imagine it's hard for her. And it's hard on you, too. I know. I lost my dad when I was young and my mom died way before then."

"Who took care of you?"

"My grandfather." He tried not to spit out the word. "He…didn't understand me, or my problems. It wasn't fun. It wasn't until I joined the military that I even found out I wasn't a complete failure. But once I figured it out, man, once I realized what I could do… It was like someone had turned on a light in the world. And I want to help you see that light. Hopefully before you're as old as I was."

Jack studied him, and then nodded, as if to say, "Yeah. You are pretty old." He didn't *say* the words, for which Luke was thankful. "What kind of stuff are we talking about here?"

"Nothing weird. I like to listen to lessons, rather than read them. But when I watch a documentary, I like it more because I can see the lesson and hear it at the same time. Maybe that's a good thing for you to try." Luke thought for a moment. "And I like to work on projects, you know, with my hands. It helps me get it. It sticks in my brain better. Stuff like that. That's what I mean by learning differently. Do you understand?"

Jack nodded.

"But there's one other reason I want to help you, Jack."

The boy stilled. "What's that?"

Luke sucked in a breath. "Well, it's your dad, Jack. I miss him so much—"

"I do, too." Something sheened in his eyes. He watched as Jack swiped at it with his sleeve.

"I want to help you as a way of thanking him for being my best friend." Oh, great. Now there was something in Luke's eyes, too.

Jack studied him for a minute. "You really liked him that much?"

"Dude, I loved him. He was like a brother to me. He was the best person I ever knew. I want to help you to grow up to be as great a man as he was." The kid didn't respond, so Luke continued. "So what do you think? You want to give this a try? See how it goes?"

The boy shrugged. "Yeah. Okay."

"Excellent." Luke thrust out his hand, and after a moment, Jack took it and they shook on it.

Chapter Five

Luke dove right into his plan of tutoring Jack. They spent the rest of Wednesday and all day Thursday and Friday together. Ironically, it was good timing because Jack was suspended until Monday. And then, when Jack went back to school, the two met in the afternoons or the evenings for their lessons.

It really touched Crystal that Luke insisted on including her in the process, making the lessons a family affair. The only hiccup was that Crystal had to work, but Luke solved that by staking out a table in the back of the B&G and setting up a makeshift classroom during her day shifts.

She suspected Luke was responding to the lecture she'd given him about the way he'd treated Jack, making sure she was aware of everything that went on, but honestly, she didn't feel the need to watch them every second. Not now. She trusted him with her son because she could tell how much Luke cared for him.

He had an interesting way of teaching. Crystal noticed it right away. For one thing, he didn't sit there and lecture Jack. He got him moving and doing things and let the learning happen organically. It wasn't a replacement for school by any means, but it was a wonderful reinforcement for the lessons Jack had struggled with in class.

And fun. There was fun, too. Luke took Jack to his family's ranch and let him drive a tractor—she thought she'd never hear the end of that one. And he took Jack fishing on the river, and then, he took him again, with his brothers and Chase tagging along because they'd heard about the trip and complained that they'd been left out.

Sometimes it seemed as though Luke was learning how to have fun again, too.

She loved watching them together. It was especially satisfying when Jack had an epiphany. He'd turn to her with a broad grin and then repeat what he'd learned in a proud voice and her heart would swell.

"You are so great with him," she said to Luke a couple weeks into the lessons. The guys had just tromped back into the house after changing the oil in her car, and Jack had gone to the bathroom to wash his hands while Luke soaped up in the kitchen sink. Her car hadn't needed an oil change, probably, but Luke said it was something everyone needed to know how to do.

"Yeah. Well, he's a great kid. Smart, too."

"Like his dad, I guess," she murmured. Then she stilled. They didn't talk about Brandon, she and Luke. It was kind of an unspoken agreement. Hopefully, she hadn't spoiled everything by bringing him up. While Luke had opened up completely with Jack, he was still a little reserved with her. She glanced at him beneath her lashes.

He blew out a heavy breath and then, to her relief, nodded. "Yeah. Yeah, he is."

She looked away, because holding his gaze was far too difficult for her these days. While she hadn't thought of a man other than Brandon for ages, sometimes, when she looked at Luke, or his hand brushed against hers, or he laughed or…breathed, she was struck with a flare of awareness. Just a flare. She never let it get beyond that. She couldn't.

Right now, this relationship was about Jack. There wasn't room for any attraction on her part. It was good to know she could still have such feelings, but that was as far as it could go. As far as it should.

She leaned against the counter and watched as

he scrubbed at a stubborn blob of schmutz. "Can I ask you something?"

"Sure."

Lord, this was hard. But it'd been niggling at her. "Why... Why didn't you come see me when you first got back?"

He stilled. A flush ran up his neck. He shrugged.

"I mean, I thought that was something buddies did for each other. I was really struggling with Jack, and losing Brandon was so hard on us—"

He stopped scrubbing, then squirted on more soap and resumed. "I was in the hospital and in rehab for two years after the explosion..."

A practiced excuse. "No. Why didn't you come see me when you first got back here? To Butterscotch Ridge?"

He leaned against the sink and flicked a glance at her. "Because I'm an ass."

Nope. Not gonna work. "That's not an answer."

He glared at her and she could see his brain desperately looking for a way out of this. Finally, he gave up and went for the truth. She knew it was the truth because she saw it in his eyes. "It was too hard, okay?" His Adam's apple bobbed. "It was too hard seeing you, because it sent me right back there." *To the nightmare.* He didn't say it, but she heard it.

The nightmare. That was what he'd been through.

Brandon had died instantly. Maybe hadn't felt a thing. But Luke... Luke had probably been lying there in the dirt howling in agony waiting for a medic. And then, when they came, they moved him. They had to move him, of course. Oh, how that must have hurt.

And even if he'd been blessedly unconscious after the explosion, he'd still woken up to the horror that his entire team had died. He was the sole survivor. There was a thing about that. Wasn't there? Survivor's guilt?

And then, of course, there was all the pain after that.

All that qualified as a nightmare, didn't it?

She shook her head. "I'm not judging, really. I just wanted to know. So, you know, I'd know." She'd cried about that for a while. Eventually she'd stopped.

He sniffed, then swiped his eye. "Well, I'm sorry I didn't. I don't know why—I mean, I came back and cut everyone off. I cut myself off. And being all alone felt right. Like a punishment I deserved, but at the same time I couldn't figure out what I'd done to deserve it."

"Grief does funny things to the mind."

He nodded slowly. "It does."

"Were you lonely?" she asked after a moment.

"No." He gave his head a little shake. Then he gave a deep, shuddering sigh and said, "Yes."

She reached for him as he reached for her and they held each other close. His warmth, the feel of his flannel shirt, the scent of motor oil and man... they all assailed her. With comfort.

"I just miss him," he whispered into her hair. "I miss him so damn much."

"I know," she said. "I know."

The moment floated around them. Until...

"Hey, Mom," Jack bellowed from the bathroom. "You're gonna have to wash the sink."

"Okay. See this? How the angles work? See how they make the structure more stable?" Luke glanced up at the top of the swing set he and Jack had just finished reinforcing. The two of them had been working together for a couple of months now when the boy wasn't in school. As Luke expected, the kid was a lot more intelligent than he'd been able to express in school. He was enthusiastic about learning, too. Even though it was a nippy December morning, they'd been at work all morning and he hadn't complained a bit.

Jack put his hands on his hips and nodded. "Yeah. By having them at forty-five degrees, the swing set won't tip over."

"Right. Great. So that's why angles are important. Tomorrow, we'll talk about angles and how to calculate distances. Once you learn that, we can talk about angles and navigation, so if you're ever lost at sea, you can find your way home."

"Lost at sea." Jack snorted a laugh. "As if."

Emma, who was sitting nearby, wrinkled her nose. "I want to learn this stuff, too," she said on a pout.

"You're a girl," Jack said.

"Girls can learn this stuff just as well as boys," Luke said quickly. "Just pay attention, sweetie, and ask questions. You'll get it in no time."

Jack didn't object, but turned his frown on Luke.

"Hey, buddy," he said softly. "You know how it feels to be left out, right?" And, when the boy nodded, Luke said, "Why don't you and Emma test the swings to make sure they work all right?"

They both perked up at that and were quickly engaged in a highest-flyer contest that Jack was sure to win—although neither really cared who won.

"Hot cocoa, anyone?"

Luke glanced up from his plans for the tree house—his next project—as Emma's mom, Lizzie, came down the yard carrying steaming mugs. She looked adorable, bundled up in her anorak, the zipper undone to accommodate her baby bump. She was due in a couple of weeks and the whole family was excited—especially Emma, who couldn't wait to be a big sister. Crystal followed closely behind with more mugs, smiling at him with a warmth that soaked through to his bones. God, she was pretty like that, in a shaft of rare winter sunlight.

"Thanks," Luke said as he took a mug and sipped. "It is a little chilly."

"It is," Lizzie said. She turned to her daughter and frowned. "Emma! Emma, honey. Not so high. Please."

Luke bit back a smile. Wait until they had a good snow and Emma wanted to toboggan down the high hill by herself! Then Lizzie would really squawk.

"We're racing," Emma hollered, and completely ignored her mom. It was wonderful, seeing her so full of energy and animation, pumping her little legs like her life depended on it.

Thank God it did not. Well, thank God, and Luke's bone marrow. And the doctors, of course. And, well, all of it. Emma was so much better than when he'd first met her. She was like a different child. But then, for that matter, so was Jack.

"Look, Mom," he bellowed as he reached the mid-upward-arc and released his hold on the chains. Both mothers gasped audibly as he flew through the air and landed on his feet. He threw out his arms and shouted, "Ta-da!"

"Oh, me! Me, too," Emma crowed, and Lizzie let out a little cry. She shoved the other mug at Luke—it spattered all over his boots—and she sprinted for Emma.

She didn't make it in time. Emma landed on her bottom before Lizzie was even close. There was complete silence for a fraction of a second, and then Emma howled...with laughter.

"Great jump, Ems," Jack said, helping her up again.

"Emma Jean. Don't ever do that again!" Lizzie wailed at the same time.

Emma chose to hear Jack. He was three years older and about a foot taller, but it was clear that she worshipped him. "Thanks." She dusted off her butt, then marched over to Luke and helped herself to the last cocoa standing. "Did you see?" she asked him in a whisper.

"I did," he whispered back. "But I think you scared your mom."

"Scared?" Lizzie huffed, because, apparently, they hadn't been whispery enough. "Try terrified." She crossed her arms. "I changed my mind. I don't think I like the swing set after all."

Luke draped his arm around Lizzie's shoulder.

"Don't you dare tell me to calm down," she snapped.

"I wasn't going to."

Lizzie glowered at him. "Weren't you?"

"Nope. I was going to ask if you wanted to try it."

"Don't be ridiculous."

"You and Crystal. How long has it been since you *played*?"

Her frown darkened. "I'm an adult."

"My point exactly."

"Luke. I'm nine and a half months pregnant. I'm not leaping out of a swing."

"I will," Crystal said. "It's been forever since I was on a swing." It wasn't long before she was flying high. And when Crystal launched herself into the air, she landed in a roll and then sat there, where she ended up, breathless and laughing so hard she cried.

Jack and Emma cheered her, too, patting her back and encouraging her with praise.

"Oh, my God," she said, laughing, as Luke hauled her to her feet. "I forgot how fun that was."

Lizzie put out a lip. "That did look like fun."

Crystal laughed. "So fun. You can try it after the baby comes."

"Maybe I will," she said with a sniff. But that was the last time Lizzie complained about the swing set.

After the moms herded the kids inside to help make lunch, Luke decided to climb up the old oak and figure out the best spot for the tree house. He kind of had an idea, but it had been decades since he'd scaled this particular tree, and trees had a habit of growing and changing over the years.

Though it hurt like hell at some points, Luke really enjoyed the exhilaration of the climb. Up and up, from one branch to the next. A month ago climbing this tree would have been a pipe dream. But, thanks to Crystal's balm, which he used daily, his muscles weren't as tight. Before he knew it, he was higher than he meant to go, high enough to see the herd grazing in the north field and the top of the barn. As a kid, he'd imagined he could see forever from here.

He and Brandon had loved climbing trees and, if
the old man hadn't been such a grouch, they would
have built a tree house right here way back when.
But Luke didn't mind doing it now. He'd do anything
for Emma. Funny how love hit a man so hard. Made
him want things.

Like a child of his own.

He shifted his hold and snorted. A child of his
own? Hah.

Yeah. Like any woman would want to get close
to *him*. But it wasn't just his physical scars that held
him back. Having an intimate relationship with a
woman—with anyone, really—meant exposing himself. Opening up and letting them see the scars on
his soul. Yeah. Any woman in her right mind would
run.

Well, hell. Why was he thinking about this? Why
not just relax and enjoy the moment? There had been
a time when he'd only been able to dream of sitting
up here again—this had seemed impossible to him
then, too.

Why not just enjoy the incomprehensible fact that,
despite his faults—and there were many—God had
seen fit to bestow a miracle on him? Granted, mir-
acles were often a result of hard work, as this one
had been, but Luke didn't think that made it any less
of a miracle. *God helps those who help themselves*,
after all. It didn't hurt that Luke was too stubborn
by far to let a little paralysis keep him from taking

that first step. And, once he'd taken that, the second and third weren't quite as hard.

He snorted to himself. What a load of crap. Every step had been hard. And they still were. But then, every painful step was a constant reminder of what he'd been able to accomplish. It was—

"Hey, Luke! Lunch is ready!" A chirpy chorus rose to greet him and he looked down to see Emma and Jack, standing at the base of the tree, peering up through the leaves.

Emma waved madly. "What are you doing up there?" she asked.

"Enjoying the view." Probably the wrong thing to say to a kid like Emma who'd been restricted from doing anything adventurous for most of her life.

"Oh," she said. "I'm coming up!"

A flare of panic lit Luke's heart...until he realized she couldn't reach the first branch. "You stay there," he called. "I'm coming down."

"But I want to!"

"I know, honey," he said as he made his way through the maze of branches. "Once we build a ladder, it'll be lots easier." And safer. "And once Jack and I build the tree house, it'll be more fun, too."

He probably shouldn't have been chattering away. He should have been paying attention to his foothold. Because one of the branches he stepped on cracked beneath his weight, and he lost his hold and plummeted to the ground with a bone-jarring thud.

He landed right on his tailbone. Pain shot through his body and his vision went red. It took a moment—okay, maybe many moments—for him to recover and, even then, every movement was torture.

Somehow, when he came back to himself, Crystal was there. Her hand was cool on his forehead, her breath fragrant. "Luke. Luke. Can you hear me?"

"Is he dead?" Emma wailed.

"He's not dead," Jack reassured her, though his voice was shaky.

No. Not dead. Just wishing he was. The pain radiated out in waves, immobilizing him. A blaze of panic whipped through his gut, a familiar horror from his days lying in a hospital bed trying to move his toes. *No*, he prayed. *Not again.*

"Just relax," Crystal said, brushing back his hair. Her voice was like a balm. "You've had a shock. Your body needs a moment."

She touched him then, on his arms and legs. His ditzy brain went straight to the gutter, which was ridiculous. She wouldn't seduce him in a situation like this. At least not in front of the kids. Would she? Yeah, it took a sec for him to realize she was checking him for broken bones.

That flash of disappointment was probably inappropriate.

"Well," she said after her inspection. "Your pupils are equal and reactive, so that's a good sign, and nothing's broken. But Luke, you really should go to the clinic and get an X-ray—"

Yeah. She'd lost him at "go to the clinic." He forced his body to sit up. The effort took all his energy, but he was able to do it. Wiggle his toes as well, thank God.

"Luke! You shouldn't move—"

"I'm fine. Fine." He showed his teeth to the kids, both of whom were gaping at him with wide eyes filled with dismay. "I'm okay. Just knocked the wind out of me. That's all." To prove it, he stood.

Oh, dear God. He should not have done that. He gripped the tree trunk as a wave of dizziness took him. "See?" he wheezed through gritted teeth. "Good as new."

Crystal snorted, but took hold of his arm and wrapped it around her shoulder, then helped him stagger to the house as though he was an old man. He definitely felt like one.

"What happened?" Lizzie asked as they hobbled into the dining room, where everyone was seated around the table. Luke winced at the mortification of them all seeing him in such a state.

"Luke fell out of the tree," Jack blurted.

Emma nodded. "It was scary."

Her mom pulled her into a hug. "I'll bet it was."

"I'm fine," he said, though none of them seemed to believe him.

Crystal helped him to his seat, then hovered. It

took a minute to realize she was gently checking his spine.

"I'm fine," he repeated. Not that he minded Crystal's touch. It was nearly comforting. But then she reached his shoulders and neck, and she touched a spot that was really tender and he yelped.

"Oh, yeah," she said, pressing harder. "You are way out of alignment, Luke. Can you feel this?"

"Yeah. It hurts," he told her.

"Mmm-hmm." She moved her fingers. "And this?"

"That hurts, too."

"Mmm. How about now?"

Damn. She pressed on another spot and the pain eased, just a little. "Better."

"Good. Listen, maybe we should go home. I can give you an adjustment."

What? No. "I'm fine. Can we just eat?"

"You're in pain, Luke."

"I'm always in pain," he snapped before he could stop himself. No one knew that. At least, he'd never said those words. Not out loud.

Crystal stepped away and came around to look in his eyes. "I can help with that," she said softly, but she didn't say anything else about it, probably because she knew damn good and well how stubborn he could be.

If he wanted help from here on out, he'd have to *ask* her for it. That much was clear.

But pain or no pain, the thought of Crystal touching him scared him to death. And he wasn't sure why.

It took all of Crystal's resources to remain clinical with Luke. When she'd rounded the corner and seen him fall...oh, Lord. She hadn't felt horror like that since... Well, it had been a long time. She never wanted to feel that way again.

Thankfully, other than a bruised tailbone, which was hardly a picnic, he seemed to be fine. She still planned to nag him about that X-ray. Just to be safe. At any rate, she watched Luke carefully all afternoon, probably just to justify her certainty that he was way out of alignment. Oh, she'd always suspected as much, given the way he walked and the way he guarded certain parts of his body as he moved. But she knew for certain, from years of training and experience, that she could help ease the pressure on the nerves causing much of his pain.

What she also knew from years of experience was that Luke Stirling was one of the most stubborn men on the face of the planet. If she was going to get him on her massage table, she was going to have to be clever.

"What are you looking at?" he grumbled as he shifted gears on the ride home; Jack, after a busy day, was asleep in the back. Luke's truck was an old beater with a manual transmission, but it was a better choice than her Saturn since the stupid heater had conked out, so when Luke had offered to drive them to the ranch for Jack's lessons, she'd jumped at the invitation.

Also, she liked spending time with Luke.

Over the last few months, their friendship had warmed, become more like it had been when they'd been The Three Musketeers—even though one of the Musketeers was gone. She knew they both still felt Brandon's loss and, at the same time, his presence.

Though she'd never mentioned it to Luke, she had noticed how he'd distanced himself from her after she and Brandon had gotten married. He'd never been cold or disrespectful to her, but that easy friendship had become a tad more rigid, as though one of them had built an emotional wall between them.

It hadn't been her.

When she'd mentioned it to Sam, she'd suggested it had something to do with a "bro code." Guys kept their distance from their friend's woman. And, since Crystal had never had brothers—or any men in her early life—she had to take Sam's word for it. With as many brothers as she had, she should know. But now, even when Brandon was dead and gone— nearly three years now—that wall was still there.

"Well?"

Crystal jerked back to the moment, to the conversation that needed to be had. "What?"

Luke blew out a sigh. "What are you looking at?"

"Your neck."

"What?"

"I'm looking at your neck."

He shot her a frown. "Why?"

She shrugged and shifted her gaze to the road, though she didn't really see it. "It's out of whack. Why wouldn't I stare?"

He reached up a broad hand and rubbed his nape. "Do I have bones poking out?"

She could tell it wasn't a real question, so she didn't answer. Her lack of response apparently annoyed him enough for him to continue the conversation, which was what she'd been shooting for.

"I fell on my butt. How would that affect my neck?"

"This may come as a surprise, but one part of your body is connected to other parts of your body."

He snorted.

"Trauma to your coccyx can have a ripple effect up and down the spine. It can cause misalignment to your neck as well as your hips, which will impact your lower body by causing you to compensate with—"

"All right. All right. I didn't ask for a lecture."

"Didn't you? But seriously, Luke, if you had appendicitis, you'd seek help."

"My appendix is gone."

"Or if you were bleeding. If you broke a limb. If you—"

"Are you going to list every possible ailment?"

"Yep." She would. She would wear him down if she had to. "Tonsillitis, water on the knee, tennis elbow—"

"Okay. Enough."

She grinned at him. "So you'll let me give you an adjustment?"

He made a noise in the back of his throat. "How long does it take?"

Really? "As long as it takes."

"Then, no."

Disappointment flooded her. "Why not?"

His glance was sharp and quick. "Because it hurts. Besides, I don't believe in back crackers."

"I am not a chiropractor. That's not what craniosacral work is. I am a *massage therapist*."

"Whatever you call it, it hurts."

"What if I promise to be gentle?" She couldn't guarantee it wouldn't hurt—because there was a certain amount of pressure required to release locked muscles and loosen tight nerves—but she could, at least, promise that.

He sighed. "Are you going to stop nagging me about this?"

"Honestly? No." She shot him a grin and was

gratified when his lips curved in reluctant response. "Your best bet is to give in and let me work on you."

"And if I hate it? Will you stop insisting?"

"Yes. I promise." Easy to say, because she knew, he wouldn't hate it. Not once he'd tried it.

So when they got to Crystal's apartment, Luke and Jack made sandwiches for dinner while Crystal set up a work area in her bedroom. Because her massage table wouldn't fully extend in her work room, and she didn't want to embarrass Luke by doing this in the living room in front of Jack, she decided to do the session on the bed, and covered the bedspread with the warming pad and a terrycloth cover. She went through her essential oils, selecting the ones best suited for muscle relaxation and pain reduction. As a therapist, she was excited to get to work on those tight muscles and help Luke live with less pain. As a woman, she was a little nervous.

Just thinking about touching his skin, massaging his flesh, flooded her body with heat.

He's a client, she reminded herself—which she'd never had to do with a client before. But she knew, it would take a lot of effort to remember that once she had him under her touch.

"You ready?" she asked Luke as Jack cleared the table and put the dishes in the sink after they'd eaten.

"No." His response was surly, and elicited a snort of a laugh from her son.

"Better get it over with," Jack advised Luke. Then he waggled the TV remote at her.

She knew what he was asking, so she nodded. "No violent stuff, please."

It was her usual mantra, but Jack surprised her by saying, "There's a show about string theory on the Science Channel."

Um… "String theory?" She glanced at Luke, who nodded.

"We're working on physics next week."

"You know," Jack said. "Einstein and Hawking. They're two of my favorites."

"Well, okay then." What else could she say? Luke had done wonders with her son. Her sense of gratitude blossomed, as did her determination to pay him back. "Shall we?" she asked as she stood.

Luke stood, too, and shot an aggrieved look at Jack, who just laughed. But he followed Crystal into her bedroom, though he paused at the door.

"Take off your shirt and pants," she said, handing him a flat sheet. "And cover yourself with this." She tried to keep her tone as clinical as she could; she didn't look at him, because that made it easier. "I'll be outside. Holler when you're ready."

When he nodded, she removed herself and closed the door, relieved to hear rustling that meant he really was stripping down and settling on the bed.

And, yeah. She tried not think about that.

The same way she'd tried not to think of Luke

in that way since the day she'd run in to him at the B&G. Not because she felt it would be a betrayal to Brandon, but because she feared taking their relationship in that direction might ruin their fledgling friendship.

As a result, she spent the better part of her days reminding herself not to think of Luke as a *man*—in a sexual sense—which, given his raw charisma and rugged good looks and the scent of him…wasn't easy. But she knew, instinctively, if she made any kind of romantic advance, he'd run—which would hurt Jack. So there you go. Friendship it was.

"Ready," he called, and she sucked in a deep breath, but before she opened the door, she sent up a quick prayer to heaven to help her remember why she was doing this…and that it wasn't to serve her own physical desires.

But damn. When she opened the door and saw him lying tummy down on her bed with the sheet casually draped over his butt, a liquid slurry shifted in her lower body and heat prickled her nape.

Stop. Just stop.

She swallowed heavily. She knew this would be hard. But she'd never expected it would be this hard. He deserved better, she reminded herself. He deserved to have all of her attention devoted to her work.

It took a tremendous effort, but she realigned her thoughts, and then began realigning his body. She began with a gentle check of his cervical spine, then a look at each vertebrae and the orientation of his hips. Finally, she checked the length of his legs.

"Hmm," she said to herself.

He raised up on his elbows. "What?"

She pushed him back down, ignoring how warm and pliant his skin was to her touch. "As I suspected, you have one leg longer than the other. About two inches, I think."

"Is that bad?"

She shrugged, even though he couldn't see. "It's fairly common. But it forces you to compensate, which puts your spine out of whack. Let's see if we can fix that. But before I start, is there anywhere that's too tender? Any spots I should avoid?"

He flushed. "Ah, this area is really tender today." He waved at his left flank. "So maybe avoid that spot?"

"No problem," she said, then went to work. It was easier, focusing on his back, easier without his eyes on her.

She started with his neck and shoulders and worked her way down. She closed her eyes and let his muscles tell her what they needed. She went slowly as she worked on his tight spots, and stayed alert to every wince and groan. A couple of times she backed off and asked, "Too much?" Each time, he shook his head.

There was a moment once—when she tugged

down the sheet and revealed a portion of his scarred side—that she felt a hot rush of emotion, a compelling desire to trace his wounds, to soothe them. But other than that, she was totally professional. Those scars though, hit her hard. They were a reminder of how he'd suffered, etched right there into his side.

As she continued working, the tightness in his body waned. His muscles released. He relaxed and leaned into her work. You could always tell when a client stopped fighting you. It was always a victory.

Perhaps it was the dissipation of tension, or the soothing scents of the oils she was using, or perhaps he'd just been struggling too hard for too long, but as Crystal was about to ask him to shift to his back, so she could work on his hips from another angle, a soft snore rumbled.

She leaned closer. Listened. And, yeah. He was asleep.

Which was unfortunate, because he was on her bed.

On the other hand, Crystal had succeeded in releasing his pain enough for him to drift off. She decided not to wake him. Instead, she covered his back with the sheet, turned off the warming pad and the lights, and slipped from the room.

"How'd it go?" Jack asked as she plopped onto the sofa beside him.

She grinned. "He's asleep."

Jack thought that was hysterical, but to Crystal, it was a win.

She knew the work she'd done would have a very real effect on Luke's discomfort, and though it wouldn't last forever—his muscles would likely tighten up as he overworked them again—at least she'd shown him that there was a way to treat his chronic pain, at least for a while.

When Jack went to bed, she popped in to check on Luke again. He'd flopped onto his side, but was sleeping so soundly, she didn't have the heart to wake him. So she grabbed a pillow and her fluffy throw, took herself into the living room and curled up on the sofa. When she finally drifted off to sleep, he featured prominently in her dreams.

Luke awoke with a heavy weight on his chest, and the sensation of tiny needles piercing his skin in a rhythmic percussion. He emerged from a dream where he was floating on a peaceful cloud in a bliss-ful, pain-free plane, so the pinpricks were especially jarring. So was the sunlight he encountered when he cracked open an eye.

Was it morning?

He stared at the window in confusion. Had he slept through the night? The whole night? Without one nightmare? How had that happened? The last thing he remembered was enduring Crystal's touch on his body with a raging hard-on, and desperately trying to think about baseball.

And what the hell was on his chest?

He forced his eyes to focus on the fat, furry creature that had taken up residence there, simultaneously purring and working its claws. On his bare skin.

Damn it. Had he fallen asleep at Crystal's again? He glanced around and cringed. In her bedroom. In her *bed.*

And, yeah. At that thought, the hard-on was back. Great. All dressed up and no place to go.

His heart skipped and he whipped his gaze to the other side of the bed. He wasn't sure why his mood dropped when he realized she wasn't there. Indeed, no one had slept there.

He'd chased her out of her own room. What a jerk.

"Come on," he said as he lifted the cat off his chest, even though it tried to make itself as heavy as possible. He stood up, tangled in a sheet, and hunted for his clothes. They were right where he'd left them, of course, and he quickly slipped them on, trying not to think about how humiliating all this was.

It wasn't until he walked to the door that he realized how different he felt.

Hell.

He rotated one shoulder, and then the other. Holy crap.

He moved his head from side to side, then back

and forth, astounded at how easy the movement was. Even his hips didn't hurt as much as usual, and he didn't stumble when he took a step.

He dropped onto the bed again and buried his face in his hands as he relished this heretofore unimaginable moment. Oh, there were still pings and twangs here and there, and his butt bone still thrummed like the devil, but he no longer felt as though he was encased in a cement suit that made movement so difficult.

A part of him wanted to dance a jig, but he knew better than that. It was still smart to go slow. Years of agony had taught him that. But still, he was humbled by this gift.

He should probably have thanked Crystal, but when he found her, curled up and asleep on her couch, he knew better than to wake her. If he did that, if he looked into her eyes feeling the way he felt…he'd do something stupid.

Like kiss her.

He'd thought of it, many times, in the past weeks. When she smiled, when she glanced at him with mischief, when she pursed her lips that way she did.

Kissing her was folly, as tempting as it was.

It would be wrong to lead her on in that way. It would be heinous to open that door when he couldn't walk though it with her. Besides, she deserved better. She deserved more than a worn-out husk of a man. She deserved better than *him*.

So he didn't wake her up. He didn't kiss her. He slipped away like a thief in the night, taking with him the precious gift she had given him and leaving nothing in return. It was a mercy, he told himself. It was a mercy to spare her from the necessity of revealing why *they* could never be. When really he was sparing himself the chore of putting that horrible truth into words.

Chapter Six

Crystal told herself it was stupid to be hurt when she discovered Luke gone in the morning. Not that she expected anything less.

Or maybe she had. Maybe she'd romanticized everything—at least in her own mind—despite her intention not to. Maybe she'd fantasized about him coming to her this morning, amazed by her talent, grateful and joyous. Maybe he might come to see her as necessary in his life. Maybe something might flower between them.

Maybe she was delusional.

Maybe he'd always seen her as a friend and never anything more. And maybe he would never see her as anything else. She should just be happy that she'd found a way to repay him for everything he was doing for Jack. Maybe that was as far as a relationship with him would go, should go.

The trouble was, since Brandon's death, no other guy made her *feel*. Made her want a relationship again. After the shock of losing her husband, she'd wrapped herself in an emotional cocoon. She'd kept her distance—not just from men, but from everyone, really. She didn't have the energy or the desire to be in a relationship. Wasn't interested in romance in the slightest.

Not until that day at the B&G when she and Luke had collided in the doorway. A switch had flipped— a wicked, naughty switch that made her *feel that way* again. In that moment, pressed against his chest, touching him, smelling him, feeling his heat… Just thinking about it made her body tingle, made her sweat.

She let go an irritated snort. For pity's sake, Jack would be up any minute. There was no time for lust. It was enough that he was helping Jack, she reminded herself. *Just be happy with what you have.*

Keeping this mantra in the forefront of her mind, she made herself a pot of coffee and watched the news as she waited for Jack to wake up.

Of course, the first thing he said to her was "Where's Luke?" The boy idolized Luke. Crystal could only hope that wouldn't end in disaster. Jack wouldn't understand Luke's need to be distant, the way she did. Jack would be crushed if Luke suddenly decided to withdraw. She needed to make sure she didn't do anything to cause that—which meant trying to maintain her emotional distance from Luke, God help her.

She shot her son an attempt at a smile. "He snuck out while we were sleeping. Again."

Jack nodded somberly. "A man needs his privacy sometimes."

"So… How are the lessons with him going?"

Jack shrugged. "Good."

Hmm. She'd hoped for more detail, but she didn't want to press. "And how about school? Any problems?"

"Nope," he said without a scrap of insecurity in evidence. Her heart lifted.

"Well, I'm glad to hear about that. Hey, I don't feel like making breakfast," she said. "Do you want to go downstairs and eat there?"

To her surprise, Jack shook his head. "Let's go to the bakery."

"Okay." Crystal's friend Veronica, who everyone called Roni for short—opened the bakery early most days. It was a good idea to visit early, before the crowd got there and she sold out of some of the best items.

Roni was newly engaged to Luke's brother, Mark, and because she used to be a teacher, Luke had roped her into helping him tutor Jack. Between Roni's understanding of Jack's challenges and her wizardry in the kitchen, she was one of Jack's favorite people right now. Eclipsed only by Luke himself.

They bundled up and made the short walk to the bakery, which still served as the only bookstore in town. And thank God it was close. There was a nip in the air. By the time they'd gone the two small-town blocks, they were both shivering. And even though the lead up to Christmas was Crystal's favorite time of year—with the decorations and lights on all the lampposts—she paid them no mind in her rush to get warm.

"Good morning," Roni said, with a stunningly bright smile, as they stepped through her door to the tinkling of the bell and a welcome blast of heat. Roni was a perky redhead with a generous heart. Jack ran to her and gave her a hug.

"He wanted to come here, rather than the B&G for breakfast," Crystal said on a laugh, unzipping her parka. "Oh, hello, Millie," she said as Roni's grandmother poked her head out from behind a shelf, to see who had come to visit. It was kind of joke around town that no one ever actually bought a book at Millie's bookstore, because she couldn't bear to let any of them go, but that wasn't true. It was only the romance novels she refused to sell.

Millie grinned…mostly at Jack. She made a beeline to him for the hug she demanded. "Good morning, young man. Look here," she said, tugging him over to a rack of superhero comics by the window. "You might like these."

Jack let out a whoop and eagerly ran to the rack. He glanced at Crystal. "May I, Mom?" he asked.

"Those comic books have been a huge hit," Roni whispered. "I'm trying to stock reading material people in this town might actually want to read. I have a whole bunch of truck magazines coming next week."

"Smart," Crystal said. Then, to Jack, she instructed, "Just be careful with them." Though, she probably didn't need to remind him to be respectful. Not now. Since Luke had come into his life, he was a completely different child. It warmed her heart.

"So how are you?" Roni asked, handing her a coffee and her favorite cream cheese pastry without even asking.

"Mmm. Thank you." Crystal took a bite—it was outrageously yummy. It took a moment to respond because she wanted the delight to linger. "Pretty good. I've been meaning to thank you for all your help with Jack. Look at him." He had selected a comic book and had settled at a table in the corner, his jacket thrown over the back of a chair…and he was diligently reading—slowly, and using his finger as a pointer. It gave her a thrill to see him beginning to find some enjoyment in the activity.

Roni nodded, her eyes bright. "That's mostly Luke, of course."

Crystal's heart pinged, just a little. "He is amazing," she said. "He is so generous with his time. And he's done wonders with Jack."

Roni's smile was warm. "Mmm. He loves helping Jack. I can tell." She chuckled. "And you have to admit, a man giving his time to a child? Well. It's really attractive, I gotta say."

"It is." But, damn, those words were hard to say. Changing the subject seemed apropos. "So," she gusted. "How are the wedding arrangements going?"

A good topic, apparently, because Roni lit up and launched into a blow by blow of all the craziness she and Mark had been dealing with. Dang. When had getting married become a full time job?

But Roni was funny and Crystal was entertained, so it was a surprise when she glanced at her watch and realized how late it was. "Hey, Jack. We have to go. I have the lunch shift today." She ignored the grumbled *aww*, the way mothers did.

"He can stay here, if you like," Roni said.

Crystal was surprised. No one had ever volunteered to look after Jack. His reputation for acting out preceded him all over town, usually leaving her high and dry. "Are you sure?"

"He can help me bake," she said loud enough for Jack to hear, then she whispered to Crystal, "We can work on fractions. Kids pay more attention when there are cookies involved."

"Well, all right. But I'm just down the street if you need me. And you, kiddo. Mind your manners, all right?"

"Okay." Jack bobbed his head like a prisoner offered a reprieve…and cookies. "I'll be so good. I swear."

"Of course, you will," Roni said with a trusting smile.

In the past, Crystal would have been leery. It always seemed to start with a trusting smile; it always seemed to end with disaster. But now, she didn't have that ball in the pit of her stomach. Now, she was pretty sure that when she came back to collect her progeny, nothing would be on fire and no one would be bleeding. There might even be baked goods.

Ah, life was good! She couldn't help but think that it was all due to Luke.

With a spring in her step, she headed to the B&G, slipped on her apron and filled up her water jug as she did every day as she prepared for work. And, as it happened, every day, the lunch rush completely sucked every crumb of her attention. Her shift flew by.

She was wiping down the bar when a sudden hush fell over the chattering crowd. She had to look up, because sudden hushes always meant someone interesting had appeared, or something interesting was about to happen. And sometimes, that "interesting thing" needed to be cut off at the pass.

Indeed, Jed Cage had just pushed through the doors, like an old-timey cowboy entering a saloon. He was wearing dusty chaps and boots and looked as though he'd just gotten off his horse after a two-day ride.

"Jed," the chorus went up throughout the bar. With the exception of the Stirlings, the Cages were the richest folks in the county. Jed typically preferred to stay on the ranch, but every time he emerged, every time he sauntered into the B&G, the same exact thing happened. Crystal bit her lip to hold back a grin as she waited for the inevitable.

Jed tipped his hat to the rapt audience as he glanced around. When he spotted Crystal, his handsome face broke into a predatory smile.

He moseyed over, his grin punctuated by the toothpick between his teeth. "Well, hello there, beautiful," he said as he leaned against the bar.

"Hey, Jed," she said, wiping down a sticky bar menu before she handed it to him. "What'll you have?"

He waggled his eyebrows, as he usually did. "Same as always."

She unintentionally snorted a laugh through her nose. He always asked for the same thing, a date with her. She knew nothing would ever come of it.

She simply wasn't interested. But still, he kept trying. "Well, you can't have *that*. How about a beer?"

Jed's bottom lip came out in a pout. "Come on, Crys. Why won't you go out with me?"

Because you call me Crys? She tried to hold back a smile. This was a familiar routine. Heck, she'd turned him down so many times it was a joke between them. "Jed, I've known you since kindergarten. You are not—nor have you ever been—serious about settling down."

His eyes went wide. "That's not fair."

"Isn't it? How many women have you dated in the last month?"

He batted his lashes and sent her a mooncalf look. "None."

"I find that hard to believe."

"It's true. I decided to hold out for you."

At this, she laughed out loud. "Good luck with that."

Suddenly, he leaned in and asked softly, "Seriously. Why do you always say no?"

She leaned toward him, too, and whispered, "You only want to date me *because* I say no."

His gorgeous face devolved into something of a pout. "That's not true."

"Plus, we're at different points in our lives." Since he'd done her the courtesy of getting serious, she thought it only fair to do the same. She wouldn't tell him the real reason, of course—that she was only attracted to Luke Stirling. Heck, no one needed to know that. "Jed, I have a son to think about now. I'm just not interested in a roll in the hay."

He sobered even more. "What if I want more, too? What if I really do want to settle down?"

She probably shouldn't have laughed, but honestly. "Jed, you go through women the way some people go through toilet paper."

She regretted the words as soon as they came out, probably because of his wounded expression. "What if I've changed?"

Had he? *Did* people change?

Jack had. Luke had. Or at least he was trying.

Crystal set her hand on his and squeezed. "If that's true, I wish you all the best, but you need to bark up some other tree. I am not the woman you're looking for."

She thought, for a second, that she'd reached him, but then his big ol' grin came out again. "Okey dokey," he said. "Maybe next time." And then, with a jaunty salute, he turned to Chase to gab about whatever it was men gabbed about when they just got shot down for the hundredth time by the same woman.

It wasn't until Crystal glanced up that she realized Luke had come into the restaurant, and he'd witnessed the entire exchange with Jed, flirting and all.

The worst part was, judging from his expression, he didn't seem to care. Not at all.

* * *

Damn. Of all the things Luke had seen in his life, that had to have been one of the most difficult. It took everything in him to remain impassive. To force a smile as he made eye contact with Crystal. But, damn, it had been hard. Even though he knew, deep in his soul, that Crystal could never be his—not in the way he wanted—it had still been a shock to see her smiling and holding hands with another man. The fact that it was Jed Cage didn't help. Jed was everything a woman like Crystal could want. He was wealthy, funny, kind and he had a face like a Hollywood actor or something. Probably not a damn scar on his whole body. No doubt, all his parts were still in factory condition. His worst injury had probably come from falling off a horse. Or getting a splinter.

Surely that wasn't jealousy roiling in his soul, that ugly, burning acid. More than likely, it was simply regret. Sometimes regret hurt more.

Or maybe it was just shock. Shock to see another man blatantly flirting with the one woman he considered untouchable.

Of course, other men would want her. Want to flirt with her, want to date her. She was gorgeous. She was smart. She had a good sense of humor.

It was wrong for him to feel this... What was it? Bitterness?

Yeah. That's what it was.

He had no business wanting her. He had no business caring who she dated. They were friends. Full stop. She'd been pretty clear about that.

He forced himself to continue across the suddenly vast room to the bar. "Hey," he said in as friendly a manner as he could muster as he reached her.

"Hey." Her smile was bright and...friendly.

"Sorry I didn't thank you for last night—" he said, then broke off when he realized what that sounded like. Heat rose on his nape. He raked a hand through his hair. "I mean..."

"I know what you mean." She set her hand on his and he tried not to think about the fact that she'd set it on Jed's, too, just moments ago. Also, they'd been flirting. He'd been able to detect that even from across the room. "I'm glad I was able to help."

He blinked. "You're not surprised?" He rotated a shoulder. "Look at this. It's amazing."

She chuckled. "I'm not surprised. I do this for money you know."

"Well, then you sure as hell shouldn't be working here." He gestured at the bar. "You should be doing that all the time. It's downright miraculous."

"It won't last forever, you know. As soon as you start overtaxing those muscles, they'll tense up again."

But he wasn't listening. "I didn't even wake up. Not once. Do you know how long it's been since I slept through the night?" He didn't give her time to answer. "Years." Three years, five months and ten days, to be exact.

"I'm glad it helped."

"Thank you." His Adam's apple worked. "I'm so glad…"

"Yes?"

He stared at her as his brain raced to find the appropriate words, raced to censor what he really wanted to say. "I'm so glad we're…friends."

Something flickered across her face, but it was gone so quickly—replaced so quickly, by her usual unruffled smile—that he had to ignore it. Her fingers tightened on his. "We are friends, aren't we?" she said softly.

He searched her expression for something—anything—that might hint to deeper feelings on her part. Of course, there was nothing—nothing but warmth and *friendship*. He nodded. "I hope so."

She nodded, too. Her smile widened. "Of course, we are." He suddenly hated the word. Even though friendship was all he could have with her, somehow he still wanted more. "Hey," she said with a burst of energy. "Why don't you come to dinner tonight?"

The quick change of topic surprised him. It took a second for him to haul himself out of that deep pit of despair and fix a smile on his face. "I'd like that…" Then his mood plummeted. *Damn.* "Oh, wait. Can't. I promised Sam I'd have dinner at the ranch. It's Danny's birthday."

"Oh." Her smile faded. "Oh, sure. Of course. Some other time then?"

"Why don't you come?" He had no idea why that came out of his mouth, other than the fact that he wanted to spend time with her. And if it had to be as friends, well, hell, *lean into it.* "Emma would love to see Jack."

"Well…okay."

It was probably unethical to use her son to emotionally blackmail her into having a meal with him, but it worked, so he decided not to sweat it. "Great. Dinner starts at six. Can I give you a ride?"

"Oh, that would be nice."

"Great." He shot her a salute and turned around to leave.

"Wait. Luke." She called him back, like a siren he couldn't resist.

"Mmm-hmm?" Was it wrong that he was thankful for one more moment with her? Or just plain ridiculous?

"Is there anything I can bring?" she asked.

This time his smile was a real one. "Nope." There was always enough food for an army. "Just yourself and Jack. I'll pick you guys up at five thirty. See you then."

"See you then," she echoed.

And, when he got to the door of the B&G, and glanced back, her eyes were still on him, and she was smiling. Which meant nothing, really. He wasn't sure why that fact lifted his mood so much, but it did.

Also, he was seeing her again tonight. That lifted his mood as well.

Danny's birthday party was raucous, but then, Crystal had expected nothing less. Especially when she walked in the door and saw the crowd. In addition to the entire Stirling family, several others were there, including Chase, his wife, Bella, and their children. Lizzie's sister, Nan, had driven over from Seattle for the weekend, and Roni was there with her grandmother, her cousins and their children as well.

It was a relief to see this wasn't strictly a family affair, because Crystal had been worried that she and Jack would stand out as nonfamily members. As it was, no one asked why they were there. Instead, they were welcomed into the fold with open arms. Sam led all the kids to the family room and put on a movie—complete with popcorn and candy—while the adults mingled and shared hysterical stories of Danny's transformation from city boy to full-on cowboy.

One of the things Crystal enjoyed the most was watching Luke respond to his siblings. It was clear he and Danny were two peas in a pod. Sam whispered to her that they'd been seriously at odds with each other when they'd first met, but looking at them now, it seemed hard to believe. They shared snarky comments and secret expressions only the two of them could decipher, as though they'd grown up together.

Luke's relationship with Sam was more complicated; most of the time she badgered him about moving back home, which, of course, made him even more adamant about staying put in town. Despite all this, Crystal could tell, at the core of it all, they loved each other deeply. Mark was so easygoing, he seemed to get along with everyone, but the interactions between Luke and his oldest brother, DJ, bothered her. There was an invisible distance between them. It was obvious in their body language, their short terse conversations and the fact that, whenever they could, the two stayed on opposite sides of the room. It must have been normal, because no one else seemed to notice.

The kids joined the adults when it was time for supper, which was followed by a fabulous cake that Roni had made. Then everyone lifted their glasses in toasts to Danny—though, again, most of the toasts had everyone in stitches.

It was a thoroughly enjoyable evening, the likes of which Crystal hadn't experienced for a very long time. It left a warm spot in her heart.

She sighed as Luke joined her in the cab of his truck for the ride home. He put the key in the ignition then turned to her. "Did you have fun?" he asked.

Though he was asking her, Jack bellowed, "Yeah!"

She made a mental note to chat with Sam about giving her son sugar, especially in the evening. But in response to Luke, Crystal simply nodded. How wonderful would it be to have a family like this?

How wonderful would it be to have the support? The sense of community? Belonging? She'd never really had it. At least, not like that. Her grandparents had raised her. They were the only parents she remembered, and they had been wonderful. But it had only been the three of them, and because they'd been much older, the family dynamic had been nothing like the explosion of energy she experienced with the Stirlings.

With Grandma and Grandpa, meals had been quiet affairs and get-togethers with friends, reserved. Their friends, of course, had been their age. There had been a lot of bridge games in their house.

Crystal hadn't even realized life could be any different until she started school and met Brandon and Luke. Not to say she hadn't enjoyed the quiet times with her grandparents, but friends her own age had taught her how to have fun. How to be silly and raucous and climb trees and fish in the pond and run barefoot in the summers.

A lot of that fun had taken place right here at Stirling Ranch, because her grandmother and Luke's grandmother, Dorthea, had been friends. Since Brandon and Luke had been joined at the hip, her husband had spent a lot of time at the ranch as a kid as well. That's how they became the Three Musketeers, although Brandon had needed to be convinced that a girl could be a Musketeer at all. Luke was the one who had insisted.

Of course he had.

She shot him a glance. His profile, limned in the blue lights of the dash, stole her breath.

She really wanted to ask him about DJ, possibly suss out the reason for the rift between them, but Jack was a little pitcher with big ears—and a bigger mouth—so she filed that conversation for later.

As they drove home, Jack regaled them with the minute details of each and every scene of the movie, which, apparently, had been about an alien robot searching for signs of intelligent life in the universe.

At one point during the monologue, Luke shot Crystal a grin. She couldn't help grinning back. It was a quiet moment, Jack's oration notwithstanding. A moment of intimacy. Of sharing. Gosh, she'd missed that, too. She had a sudden urge to reach across the bench seat and take his hand. But she thought better of it and curled her fingers into her palm instead.

Naturally, she spent the rest of the ride regretting her choice and calling herself a coward. So when he pulled up at her place—after Jack had bounded out—she turned to him. "Do you want to come in for a cup of coffee?"

He blinked. "It's late, isn't it? Aren't you working the early shift tomorrow?"

She nodded. "I noticed you were limping a little today. I thought could give you another adjustment."

To her surprise, he agreed. "You know what? That would be great. If you're sure…"

The intensity of that flare of delight—of satisfaction, excitement and possibly savage validation—surprised her. She hid it well. "Okay then," she said as she opened the door and slipped out of the truck.

"Okay then," he said as he followed suit; she noted a lightness in his tone and that made her feel happy as well.

Though Jack was so tired he seemed dizzy, he refused to go to bed until Luke told him a story about his dad. Meanwhile, Crystal set up her massage table in the living room. It was far better than massaging Luke on *her* bed, simply because last time, doing so had given her some very naughty thoughts.

Not that she had anything against naughty thoughts—she had them quite often about him. It was the juxtaposition of her work with such naughty thoughts that made her uncomfortable. She needed to focus on healing, not how great his body felt beneath her hands.

And it did feel great. Amazing. Hard and warm and—

Damn it!

She closed her eyes and gritted her teeth. Yep.

She needed that table here. She needed the reminder that this was *work*.

But when he came into the living room, and he asked why they were using the massage table, she said, "The height gives me better angles." Technically, not a lie. It also had a firmness the bed couldn't match.

But she probably shouldn't think about firmness in this situation, should she? Especially as he unbuttoned his shirt and bared his chest. He was shy about shedding his jeans, and made her turn around until he was settled on the massage table and under the sheet.

"So," he said so suddenly it made her jump. "How did you get into massage therapy?"

She turned around to find him settled on the massage table, face down, with the sheet draping his hips. She tried to ignore the fact that she could still see his butt, outlined as it was by the thin sheet.

Luke's buttocks were perfectly shaped, layered with muscle and…

Oh, dear. Was she drooling?

"Crystal?"

"Huh?" What had he asked? "Oh. Yeah. Well, I always gave my grandmother massages. You remember how hard it was for her to get around?"

"Mmm-hmm."

"I've always been very good at it, and I enjoyed it, so I decided I was going to open Butterscotch

Ridge's first and only massage therapy clinic. Took courses online and got my certification and everything."

"And what happened?"

She stilled. Surely he knew what had happened? "When Brandon died, everything imploded. Jack and I lost the house and suddenly I needed a job to put food on the table."

He lifted his head slightly, his tone growing remorseful. "I am so sorry, Crystal. I should have known."

"It's okay." She shrugged. "Chase stepped in. He's great."

"He is."

"Besides, that was years ago, you know? Not that I don't think about Brandon every day and miss his laugh and his smile. It hits me sometimes at random times."

"I know what you mean."

She sighed. "Well, enough of my maudlin stories. Are you ready to begin?"

"Yes, please."

"All right." She lowered the lights, turned on the soothing music and set to work.

His shoulders were much looser than last time, and most of the kinks in his upper body released easily. His hips took a bit of effort. She asked him to roll onto his back so she could work to address the tightness in his lower back that was shortening the muscles in that one leg.

This pressure could be painful, and Crystal knew, from his response, that Luke felt it.

"You okay?" she asked.

"Mmm-hmm," he said on a groan.

"Should I stop?"

He shook his head. "Keep going. I know it'll feel better when you finish."

"Sure." She shot him a smile, but realized too late that because of her position over him, they were closer than she'd thought. She was entranced by the lines on his face. Fascinated by the tiny tears at the corner of his eyes. Enraptured by the perfection of his lips.

When his tongue peeped out, just for a second, between those perfect lips, a shock wave rocked her. It took everything in her to step back. To move away from him. To not look at the lower portion of his body that was so ineffectively covered by the sheet.

"Almost done," she said, as she took the position at the top of the bed to gently manipulate his cervical spine from beneath. This was more awkward than usual, because when she glanced down at him, his eyes were on her...well, on her breasts.

It was irritating, the way that excited her. When he noticed that *she* noticed where his attention was, he closed his eyes. She continued her work. She should be satisfied that he was feeling pleasure, judging by his soft moans. It just wasn't the kind of pleasure she might have liked.

She had no idea why such sadness swamped her. Well, perhaps she did. Of course, she did.

She was lonely. Painfully, achingly lonely and he was the only man she was even remotely attracted to. No wonder she was sad and frustrated and—

Well, hell. She shouldn't have allowed herself to go there. Or she should have quietly left the room before the tears welling in her eyes fell. But one splattered on his cheek, and by then, it was too late for her to escape. He sat up quickly—faster than he should have after an energetic realignment—and grabbed her by the arm as she tried to turn away, spinning her so that she faced him. And then, to her utter horror, he lifted a hand to her face and wiped away her tears. His callused fingers were rough on her skin. It felt so good, so warm, so protective…it made her cry harder.

"What is it?" he whispered, gently easing her closer to him, pulling her hair from her face, then tipping up her chin so she was utterly exposed. "What's wrong?"

She couldn't answer, other than to shake her head, because his gentleness launched yet another raft of uncontainable sorrow. How could she tell him without embarrassing herself? Without ruining their friendship? How could she admit what she wanted, when she was pretty sure it had never crossed his mind? And, if it had, he'd rejected the idea. How humiliating would it be to hear him explain that he didn't want her?

"Crystal, please." He shifted his hands and cupped her cheeks, stared into her eyes with an empathy that humbled her. "Talk to me."

Suddenly, her emotions veered to the right and morphed into something like anger.

Why should she have to pretend? So what, if he didn't want her? If that ruined their friendship, it wouldn't be her fault. It would be his, damn him, if he couldn't handle it. If he abandoned Jack because of it, it wouldn't be on her. It would be his fault. She frowned at him, putting all her anger and frustration into that one glare.

He blinked, probably in surprise. He'd never seen this side of her before. For him, she'd always pretended. Around him, she'd always stuffed down her emotions. Around him, she'd always acted as though her feelings for him were sisterly. So this had to be throwing him for a loop.

She'd always been faithful to Brandon, because she believed fidelity was what marriage was about, but it would be a lie to say she hadn't been attracted to Luke. Something had always sparked in her soul when he came into a room. She had always chosen to interpret that feeling as deep abiding friendship. Lifelong friendship.

Yeah, she'd gotten good at pretending. The trouble was, she'd pretended so well, she'd even convinced herself that she had nothing but a doting admiration for her dead husband's best friend.

She knew now, in his arms, what a raging lie that was.

But now, pretending wasn't necessary. Brandon was dead. He'd had been buried and mourned.

She was alive. And she was tired of pretending. She was tired of trying to protect a secret that no longer needed to be kept.

And if Luke didn't like it, well, to hell with him.

So she did the thing she'd been aching to do—for years, if she was being honest.

She kissed Luke Stirling.

Chapter Seven

She caught him by surprise. The last thing he'd expected was for her to lean forward and touch her lips to his. And, ah… She tasted like, well, heaven. Sweet and bright with a hint of salt—probably from the tears. They only heightened his sensations, the way salt makes sweetness sweeter.

And, God, she was sweet. Alluring. Soft. Warm. All the good things in life.

A part of his brain insisted this shouldn't be happening…for so many reasons. But there was another part of his brain that wanted it, wanted this, so badly he couldn't resist.

Hell. Let the future take care of itself. For now, for this moment, he wanted only her.

When he wrapped his arms around her and pulled her closer, she groaned, then she tipped her head and deepened the kiss. He nearly came out of his skin when she touched her tongue to his. Pleasure speared him. Similar delight danced through him as she touched his chest, at first with her palm, and then with trailing fingers. Down and down…

He was so lost to the glory, to the feel of her painting pleasure on his chest, that he almost didn't stop her in time.

It was thoughts of Brandon—his best friend, his loyal brother in arms—slamming into him, filling him with shame and self-disgust, that moved him to catch her wrist gently.

She pulled back to look at him, her expression one of dazed confusion.

He knew in his heart the moment had come, the moment to tell her the truth and unburden his soul.

God, he didn't want to. He didn't want to. But she needed to know. She deserved that much, at least. Didn't she?

What a shame it was that his courage failed him.

Crystal's breath caught as she stared at Luke.

He was going to kiss her again. He was going to pull her back into his arms and hold her close and love her the way she hungered to be loved. She knew it, just knew it to the core of her being. Delight and anticipation and impatience warred within her; her head spun with delirium.

But no. That was lack of oxygen. She reminded herself to breathe, and exhaled on a bit of a laugh.

It was then that she noticed a change in him, a bracing of muscles, a tightening of the tiny lines around his mouth, the sudden chill.

She tried to pull her wrist from his hold, but he wouldn't allow it. He captured her gaze, and with it, held her prisoner. "Crystal," he said in a tone that made her shiver, made her chest ache. "We can't."

He said no more than that, but spoke with such finality, she couldn't pretend it was anything other than rejection. Not rejection of her—the passion in his eyes made that clear. It was a rejection of this. Of them.

"Why?" A simple question, nearly a whisper, asked with a rawness that hurt.

His response was to step away, dress quickly, enrobe himself with that invisible barrier once more.

"Luke?"

Though he was halfway to the door, he stopped and turned and stared at her. And then, he said a terrible thing. A thing no one really wants to hear because it's trite beyond bearing. "It's not you, Crystal. It's me."

Really? She stared at him, rendered speechless by a lethal combination of bone-deep loss and a bubbling irritation. She hadn't realized, until now, that she'd slid so far into the fantasy. That, despite all her denials, she'd bought in to the fairy tale—hook, line and sinker. It took a great deal of fortitude, but she swallowed those battling emotions and forced herself to feel nothing. Or, at the very least, *show* nothing.

She put back her shoulders and smiled…or something like it. "I understand."

He blinked. "Uh, you do?"

"Of course." She turned her attention to folding up the sheet so she wouldn't have to look at him. "Brandon was your best friend." When he didn't respond, she glanced at him with an arched eyebrow. "You feel guilty."

His nod was minuscule, his face sallow. "I do. It feels…wrong."

"Yeah," she said on a sigh. "I get it." She'd suspected it all along. She'd felt the guilt as well. But she'd convinced herself that Brandon wouldn't have wanted her to be alone. Wouldn't have wanted Jack to grow up without a strong male influence. It had made sense for Luke to fill that role. He'd loved Brandon. She liked to believe he loved Jack. She'd hoped he'd come to love her.

Though she wanted to rail, though she wanted to holler and break things, this wasn't the time. Though it was disappointing to learn that Luke had no interest in a deeper relationship with her, or was too guilt-ridden to step into a romance with his best friend's once-wife—and what was the difference, really?—she had to honor his feelings.

Yes. She loved Luke Stirling and always had. She respected him and liked him, too. Now that he was in her life, she really couldn't imagine it without him. A certain part of her soul knew that the only way to keep him in her world, and Jack's, was to play along. To keep her emotional self silent and play along. She had to keep her mitts to herself and bury her desire for him.

In short, pretend.

Fortunately, she had lots of practice.

It cost her a lot to smile in his general direction. "I understand, Luke. I do. Let's make a pact, shall we?"

"A pact?"

"We'll always be friends, no matter what. Okay? No secrets, no guilt."

"No...sex?"

She wasn't sure if this was a suggestion or a term he was proposing, but it hardly mattered. "It takes two," she said. "If you don't want to go there—"

"It's not that I don't *want* to—"

"I know. If it's not something you're comfortable with..." She glanced at him and waited until he nodded. "Then we won't." She tightened her resolve, for Jack's sake, even though being this close to Luke made her drool. "I really need you in my life, Luke. I'm sorry if I said or did anything that made you—"

"Stop. Please stop." He pulled her into his arms

and held her. It felt so wonderful, she had a hard time reminding herself it wasn't the kind of hug she wanted it to be. She'd have to work on that. Might take a century or so. "You didn't do anything wrong. Neither of us did. And, frankly, I need you in my life, too." He gave a little laugh that resonated through her body. "And Jack."

"Then that settles it." She leaned back and stared up into his beautiful, ravaged face. "We will be friends."

He smiled. It even reached his eyes. "Thank you, Crystal." When he took her in his arms and hugged her, she tried not to sigh. This was the way it would be, from now on. She had to find a way to reshape her expectations around Luke. Around her life. It was time to let go of her hopes for something deeper with him. It was time to move on.

Luke left Crystal's apartment hurting and numb. *Damn it all. Damn it all, anyway.*

He thought about heading down to the B&G and getting epically plastered, but the last time he'd done that, it hadn't turned out so well. So he headed home instead. It was a shame he didn't have anyone to talk to. None of his family or friends had a clue that he'd been harboring a secret crush for Crystal since high school. No—junior high?

That was the problem with keeping secrets.

You held them alone. Utterly alone.

Luke let out a harsh laugh. He'd spent most of his life feeling alone. This was nothing new. Not really.

Except he'd never wanted like this. Never wanted so badly to be un-alone. And she was the one he wanted to be un-alone with.

Yet, he'd stopped her.

Thank God she hadn't been offended or angry when he'd stopped her. Thank God she hadn't cut him right out of her life. They were still friends. They could still spend time together. That was something he could hold on to, at least.

But for now, he was just a guy in love with the girl his best friend had married. Was there anything sadder?

Yes. Yes, in fact, there was. And Luke knew exactly what it was.

He let himself into his place, made a beeline to his albums and dug out the Mozart Requiem—widely touted as the saddest piece of music ever composed. But not even halfway through it, he had to turn it off with a self-directed scoff because, damn, this was beyond sad. This was maudlin. He'd never been much of a wallower and this—this felt like wallowing.

The fact of the matter was, he was damn lucky. He'd cheated death, he could walk on his own two feet, he had his health, he was able to serve others with the gifts God had given him and he found great joy in music, friendship and flying.

It was a rich life. It was a good life.

Was it wrong to want more? He hoped not, because he did. Despite everything, he wanted more. He wanted more with her.

For a second, his mind spun with thoughts of where he'd be, what they'd be doing right this moment, if he hadn't stopped her. But somehow, even imagining it dredged up self-reproach bitter enough to turn his stomach.

She was Brandon's wife and, yeah, Brandon was dead. Somehow, in his heart and soul, she was still Brandon's wife, and always would be. He wished he could just slough off that mindset. But he didn't know how.

Especially since he was the reason Brandon was dead. And taking his woman… Well, that was plain wrong.

"Well, someone's lost in thought."

Crystal jerked up when she realized Lizzie was talking about her. It was true. She'd been sitting with her friends in the heated gazebo just past the rambling lawn behind the Stirling house, which had been decked out for the coming holiday. The kids played in the snow that had fallen last night, while she replayed that conversation with Luke in her mind… again. "Sorry." She readjusted her gloves, just for something to do.

She was not unaware of the look Roni and Lizzie shared. "Is, uh, everything okay?" Roni asked.

"I'm fine," she said with a smile, taking a sip of coffee from her thermal mug. "Just a lot on my mind, I suppose."

"How's it going with you and Luke?" Lizzie asked.

The question was so unexpected, Crystal snorted coffee through her nose; it was so painful, her eyes watered. "I, ah, what?"

Lizzie blinked. "Sorry. I thought you two were a thing."

"Me, too," Roni said. "I mean the way he was looking at you at Danny's party…"

"We're friends." She even managed to flash them a smile. She was very proud of herself.

"But he was *really* looking at you." Lord, Lizzie could be insistent.

"Don't you find him attractive?" Roni asked.

Heat washed through her. Frustration, too. The mix was becoming all too familiar.

Yeah. Luke was attractive. There was no doubt about that. But… "We're just friends. We see each other a lot because he's tutoring Jack."

"He has seemed much calmer lately," Lizzie said. "Jack, I mean. Not Luke." She gave a laugh.

"Jack has always been well-behaved around me," Roni said. But she was once a teacher. She probably knew a magic spell or something. Or maybe it was the way she treated Jack with respect and patience that put him in her thrall.

"Luke has been showing Jack some of the tricks he learned to deal with his dyslexia."

Roni smiled. "He brings him by to help at the bakery."

Lizzie tipped her head to the side. "Really?"

"Yes." Roni leaned in. "Baking is very scientific. Practically a chemistry lesson. With cookies."

"Jack really enjoys those visits," Crystal said with a grin.

"Yeah." Roni sighed. "Luke really is a really good teacher. I think he missed his calling."

"He likes being a handyman." Crystal felt the urge to add that fact, as though she had any right to defend his choices.

"He's spending more time at the ranch lately," Lizzie mused. "Thank God. I'm getting tired of listening to Sam grouse about the fact that he lives in town."

"He seems to like his privacy." Dang. There she went again. Defending his choices.

"So here's what I don't understand…" Lizzie paused, and both Crystal and Roni turned to her expectantly. Lizzie grinned like the Cheshire cat. "If you like him and he likes you…why are you just friends?"

Crystal sighed. "Can't you guess?"

"No." Lizzie set her chin on her hands and blinked her eyes. "Do tell."

"It's hard to talk about…"

"It's Brandon," Roni blurted.

"Yeah." Crystal nodded at Lizzie's disbelief.

Lizzie frowned. "Did he tell you that?"

Had he? She couldn't remember what he'd actually said, only the way it made her feel. "We had a conversation about it. He made his feelings pretty clear."

"Oh, honey." Roni hugged her. "I'm so sorry."

While it was nice to have someone to commiserate with, it revealed a vulnerability you didn't have to face when you kept everything to yourself. It was much easier to pretend when no one else knew your secret.

Lizzie shrugged. "Well, I don't know what to say. Usually at this juncture, I'd make a comment about what an idiot he is, and you're better off without him—"

"And there are other fish in the sea," Roni added.

"But this is Luke. Other than being stubborn, I can't find too many faults in him," Lizzie said. "Why couldn't you have fallen for someone who's easy for your friends to hate?"

Heat rose on Crystal's face. "Did I say I've fallen for him?"

Lizzie gusted a sigh. "The mooning gave you away."

Roni nodded. "Dead giveaway."

"Rats. Well, there you go. Sad story that it is…"

"That he's loyal to his best friend?" Lizzie shook her head. "There's honor in that. I suppose."

"Do you really think that's all it is?" Crystal sat up in her lounger to face them both. "I mean I made it pretty clear that I was wide open to taking this to the next level. *He* stopped it."

Roni glanced at the kids; Jack had just landed on his butt in a snowdrift and Emma was laughing gleefully. "Maybe he was worried about what Jack would think?"

"Then he would have said so." Of all the things Crystal knew about Luke, the fact that he said what he thought was at the top of the list. Of course, he would probably never just come out and say, "Crystal, you're just not my type," but part of her wished he would. It would make things easier. For her, at least. That was the only other reason he'd turn her away. Wasn't it?

"You know what you should do?" Roni said. "You should go out on a date with someone else."

Oh, God. "No."

"Wait…" Roni leaned closer. "Didn't you tell me Jed Cage asked you out?"

"Yes." About a hundred times.

"Ooh." Lizzie's eyes went wide. "You should go for it!"

"That's not fair to Jed, is it?" Crystal asked. "I'm really not interested in him."

Roni narrowed her eyes. "Have you ever gotten to know him?"

Crystal huffed a laugh. "I went to kindergarten with him."

"That doesn't count. People change."

"Honestly, no. I mean, Brandon and I started dating in junior high school. He's the only one I even thought about…" Other than a silly schoolgirl crush on Luke. And it hadn't been until he'd walked back into her life that those feelings had come roaring back, ten times hotter, damn it.

"You should try, at least," Roni said.

When Crystal shook her head and started to object, Lizzie interrupted her. "Do you want to be single for the rest of your life?"

"I… No." No, God, no. It crystallized before her, this imaginary future where she sat in a rocking chair on a porch somewhere, all alone and yet still surrounded by feral cats. "No."

Lizzie shrugged. "Then you've got to try. How else will you know, right?"

Though she was pretty sure she wouldn't—and mostly to make them stop nagging her—Crystal agreed.

She got her chance to chat with Jed sooner than she expected. That night while she was working, he meandered into the bar. As she watched him coming, she tried to see him with a fresh perspective.

He was handsome—that had always been obvious. He was tall. He had a nice smile and a playful glint in his eye. There was nothing wrong with Jed. Nothing that she could put her finger on...other than the fact that he wasn't Luke.

Oh, all the women in town chased after him—he was considered one of the most eligible bachelors in the county now that Mark Stirling was off the market—but he'd never acted like an arrogant jerk. He was even able to laugh at himself, which Crystal found particularly attractive in a man.

"Hey, beautiful," he said as he sidled up to the bar. "How are you doing?"

"Just peachy," she said, wiping off the sticky bar menu and handing it to him. Chase'd had them laminated, but they were always mysteriously sticky. "What can I get you?"

He grinned and waggled his eyebrows. "You know what I want. When are you going to break down and say yes?" Gosh, his grin really was gorgeous.

It took a second to steel her spine and take her friends' advice. Kind of. "What would you do if I did?"

He stilled and stared at her for a second, then he really turned on the grin. It was blinding. "That's not a no. Am I finally wearing you down?"

She blew out a breath. "Believe it or not, I'm thinking about it."

He let out a whoop that echoed through the restaurant. Conversations stopped. Heads swiveled.

"Shh!" she hissed. "Have you forgotten where we live?"

To which he hooted a laugh. "Do you seriously think something like this would ever be secret? In this town?"

She knew it would not. "I don't like people talking about me."

He chuckled. "Have you forgotten where we live?" And then, when he sensed she was backing out of an almost yes, he added, "We could go somewhere else. This isn't the only restaurant in the world, you know."

"Isn't it?" It was a lame attempt at a joke, but he still laughed.

He picked at a spot on the bar. "Of course, even if we went to the moon, someone around here would find out. It's probably better just to face it head-on."

"Oh, you're right." It would be easier. Wouldn't it? Besides, it was just one date. One meal. No promises or anything.

He paused for a second, then asked, "So what do you think? Will you go out to dinner with me? Tomorrow night?"

Her heart leaped. "So soon?"

"Why wait?"

"I have Jack—"

"Can you get a sitter?"

Oh, why had she said yes? Had she said yes? "I suppose. I mean, I can try."

"Awesome." He wasn't going to give her a chance to back down. "How about I pick you up at six?"

Oh, Lord. How long had it been since a man asked her out? What was she even supposed to wear? "I... maybe it's not a good idea."

"Ah-ah-ah." He waggled a finger. "None of that."

"Jed, I..."

"Okay. We'll have dinner here. Right here. You'll be in a familiar place, surrounded by people you know."

Somehow, that did make her feel better. It was certainly better than driving to the Tri-Cities. Or flying to the moon. "All right." She said it quickly, before she chickened out. "Tomorrow night. Here. Six o'clock."

"Awesome. It's a date."

She had a date. A date.

Oh, God. What had she done?

When Luke woke up, the day after his second massage from Crystal, he was refreshed, full of energy and feeling pretty damn good. He'd only had one nightmare, and for a change he'd been able to slough it off and go right back to sleep.

He'd expected to lie awake all night, thinking

about that awkward conversation with Crystal, but he hadn't, and now he felt pretty good about their chat. Their relationship could just go on as it was with his honor intact. Nothing would change. It would be perfect.

And that little niggle, deep in his soul? The little voice that cried for more with her? That, he could ignore. Couldn't he?

He spent most of that day at the church, fixing the heater again, then headed out to the ranch to help DJ and Mark feed the herd. As he fell into bed that night, he was tired, but it was a pleasant ache of muscles well used. He didn't know how Crystal did it, and he didn't care. All he knew was how much he appreciated her.

The next day, after he finished fixing some tiles on the roof of the church's homeless shelter, he headed to the B&G for lunch with Fred and AJ, a couple of his fellow vets, and—if he was being totally honest—to see Crystal again. He was bummed that she wasn't working, and didn't answer when he knocked on her door upstairs. He wasn't sure why that made him feel desolate—he'd seen her just the day before yesterday. But she'd become part of his life, he supposed. He missed her. It was ridiculous to feel this way, of course, so he tried to ignore it. He hopped in his truck and headed to the ranch to work on the tree house for a while, because building gave him pleasure and he wanted to at least get the

frame up before the snowstorm racing down from
Canada hit.

When he pulled into the driveway, his heart
jumped because he noticed Crystal's old Saturn in
the lineup of cars. He spotted her as soon as he came
through the front door, as though he had a radar
for her or something. She was down the hall at the
kitchen table in the middle of an intense discussion with Lizzie and Sam. They were all close and
whispering so intently, they didn't notice him arrive.
He was about to head that way, but Emma's chirpy
voice caught his attention and he paused in the hall
at the front room.

Apparently, a tea party was in full swing, with
his grandmother, Emma and Jack in attendance,
but Grandma was asleep. Ignoring her loud snores,
Emma and Jack were engaged in a heated conversation as well, but there wasn't much whispering as
neither of them had really mastered voice modula-
tion.

"I don't know," Emma said in that bright chirp,
while pouring invisible tea from a plastic pot into
Jack's plastic cup. The scene was heartwarming for
so many reasons, not the least of which was the fact
that Jack was playing along, even sipping from the
empty cup. Emma handed him a plate piled with
cookies. The cookies, it should be noted, were real.
"I didn't have a daddy for a long time, either. Then

one day—poof!—he just showed up. Maybe your daddy will just show up, too."

Jack sighed and brushed back his bangs. They flopped right back down. "I don't think so. My dad died. I don't think he'll just appear like that."

"Oh." Emma patted his hand and then selected a cookie for herself. "Well, maybe you can get a new one."

"Mom says we don't need one," Jack said, in a declaration that made Luke's chest hurt for some reason. "We don't need anyone. *We are all fine by our own selves.*" Luke could only assume this last bit was meant to be his mother's voice, because he said it in falsetto.

Emma contemplated her cookie for a long while, and then said, "Well, you can borrow my dad if you need one." She shrugged. "He's pretty good."

Jack nodded solemnly. "Thanks."

"Luke!" Sam's bellow from the kitchen caught everyone's attention. The kids both jumped up and ran to him while the women turned to stare at him as though he was a rare animal wandering into their midst.

"Hey, everyone," he said, making his way to the kitchen table with Jack at his heels and Emma in his arms.

"Luke." Sam again. He had no idea why she looked so solemn, but he had the sudden urge to run.

"Are you hungry?" Lizzie asked. *She* was polite.

"Starving." As he took off his fleece jacket, he smiled at them all. One more than the others. "Hey, Crystal."

"Hey, Luke." God, she looked pretty today. Her hair was back in a ponytail, the way she usually wore it at work. Her nose was spattered with freckles. Her lips were… He ripped away his gaze.

As he put down Emma and settled himself in his chair, Lizzie fixed him a plate of fresh fruit, veggies and something that might have been tofu. Not his favorite food in the middle of a busy day, but he was hungry, so he tucked in, hardly making a face at all. Crystal, of course, noticed it and shot him a smile.

"It's good for you," she murmured.

"It's a good thing I'm hungry," he responded with a wink. While he ate—everything but the tofu—the women continued their conversation.

"So, what are you going to wear?" Sam asked.

For some reason, Crystal glanced in his direction, then flushed. "I—I don't know. It's been so long…"

"What's the occasion? Oh, Mark and Roni's wedding?" Luke asked through the chunk of juicy pineapple tickling the sides of his tongue.

"Nope." Sam leaned forward. "Crystal has a date."

Something jerked in Luke's chest and he began choking on the pineapple he'd just swallowed. As he recovered, he stared at Crystal, mind befuddled, heart bereft. She, of course, looked away, unfazed by his agony.

And how ridiculous was his agony? She'd made damn clear she wanted something more with him the last time they'd spoken...and he'd made damn clear that there could be nothing but friendship between them.

Of course, she would date other men. Of course, she would marry again—

The acid in his gut rebelled against the thought.

It was totally unfair of him to expect her to remain alone.

But that didn't make it hurt any less.

Chapter Eight

Sam nudged Luke's foot under the table. "Aren't you going to say anything?"

What did they expect? *Please, don't do it?*

"Ah, who is it?" It was the first thing that came to mind. After "please, don't do it," of course.

Sam frowned. "Jed Cage."

Luke arched an eyebrow at his sister. "The guy who took you to prom?"

Lizzie gasped. "He took you to prom? Jed Cage? Why didn't I know that?"

Sam's frown turned into a glower. "I only said yes to piss off the old man." She turned to Lizzie. "He hated the Cages."

Crystal chuckled. "I forgot about prom." Why the hell was she laughing? None of this was *funny*.

"Easy to see why you'd forget," Sam said with a hint of bitterness. "Jed dated nearly as many women as Mark since high school." Their brother had been a known Lothario, though he'd settled down happily since falling in love with Roni. Or Roni's baking. Hard to tell.

Surely a serial dater wasn't the right kind of guy for a single mother. But who was he to judge? It wasn't his business. It couldn't be.

"How do you feel about this?" Luke asked Jack.

The boy made a face. "I told her I wanted you to date her instead."

For some reason, this eased the sting. He tried not to smile, but must have because when he caught Sam's gaze, she smirked. When he glanced at Crystal, she was red as a lobster.

"Why would you date anyone but Luke?" Emma asked, hugging his arm. He lifted her onto his lap.

"Well…" Crystal began as though choosing her words carefully. "Jed asked me out." And she left it there.

Jack frowned at Luke. "Why didn't *you* ask her out?"

The same thought whipped through him like a sirocco, even though he knew the damn answer.

"Emma Jean," Lizzie said, in a sudden gust. "Did you tidy up after your tea party?"

"Aww, Mom!"

"We've talked about this, honey. You have to clean up after you play. Other people live here, too."

"I'll help," Jack said, taking her hand. "Come on. It'll be fun."

As the two left, Jack shot a stealthy wink at Luke and his heart warmed just a little. Because the kid had been listening to him. And now he was passing on the things he'd learned to Emma. It was kind of cool if you thought about it.

His hubris was short-lived, though, because he caught a glance of Crystal in the corner of his eye and remembered, all of a sudden, what they'd been talking about.

Her date. With Jed.

"So," he asked as nonchalantly as he could. "When is this…date?"

When she said, "Tonight," it was like a cannonball to the gut.

"So you'd better decide what to wear," Lizzie urged.

"It's just at the B&G," Crystal said, taking pains not to look in Luke's direction. "Maybe my black dress?"

The women both nodded. "Can't go wrong with a black dress," Lizzie said.

"He's taking you to the B&G?" For some reason, Luke blurted this out, even though he'd had no intention to do so. "Fancy."

Ooh. She looked at him now. It was a scolding frown. "He wanted me to feel comfortable."

Lizzie nodded. "Of course. You were nervous. It was a romantic gesture. That's sweet."

Sam snorted a laugh and, when they all looked at her, she shrugged and muttered, "Well, at least you know what's on the menu." Then, in case anyone missed her jest, she added, "Because you work at that restaurant."

Crystal sighed. "The point of the date is for me to get to know him better. To give him a chance, like we talked about." Luke frowned. She hadn't talked to *him* about it. "Not some fancy-schmancy dinner with roses and violins."

"You're right." Lizzie patted Crystal's hand. "You're just exploring. This isn't a commitment." *Good.* "Although, you never know where romance will blossom. And he is… Well, he is handsome."

Luke snorted at that. Probably because it was true, damn it all, anyway.

"So, do you have a sitter?" Lizzie—the only other mom at the table—asked.

Crystal cleared her throat. "I was going to ask one of you…"

"Oh, I'm busy," Sam said definitively.

"What the heck are you doing tonight?" Lizzie asked—they both lived in the same house. Sam just narrowed her eyes.

"It won't go late, I promise. Just—"

"I'll do it." Again, the words just came out. They surprised even Luke. But what the hell. Why not? He and Jack got along. There was plenty they could do. And, frankly, it wasn't a bad idea to be there when Jed brought her home. Just to let him know someone was looking out for her. Just to be sure no monkey business occurred.

When Crystal shook her head and said, "You don't need to do that," it only made him more determined.

"I'm doing it," he said in his firmest voice. He was doing it, and that was that.

And it was only partly because he liked spending time with Jack. The other part of him wanted to make damn sure Jed knew that this small family was under Luke's wing.

It was a little awkward that night when Luke arrived to stay with Jack, although Crystal wasn't sure why. They'd agreed on friendship. He'd insisted on it. So why did she have the weird sense that he was annoyed that she was going out with Jed? There was no reason for him to care if he didn't have that kind of interest in her.

In the end, she just chalked it up to protectiveness. The way a brother protected a sister from a virile man, perhaps.

Jack's pouting was a lot easier to figure out. He liked Luke, and didn't understand why she would go out with Jed. "You don't need that guy when Luke's right here. Luke is perfect." Even though Crystal told him, again and again, that she and Luke were just friends, it wasn't enough to convince him. Maybe because she wasn't completely convinced, either.

Even though she was excited getting ready for her date, she had to admit, she was most excited about seeing Luke. Indeed, when he came through the door and saw her in the black dress with makeup on and everything, he stopped short, as though stunned, and stared at her. His expression, however, was inscrutable. She had no earthly clue what that muscle ticking in his cheek meant.

She expected him to say something about her dress or her hair, but he didn't. She was silly to have expected it. For her—at least—the moment was awkward. Fortunately, Jack was there to break the tension, as he greeted Luke with a whoop, then took the bags from his hands and rushed into the kitchen.

"Hey," Luke called. "Don't go through that. I want it to be a surprise."

Jack issued one of his "awws," but Crystal could tell it was just for show. She liked how he respected Luke, and obeyed him. That in itself was a minor miracle.

He leaned in and whispered, "I brought a science project. And hot dogs."

"He'll love that. And thank you for doing this," she added as the silence threatened to swallow them up.

"What? Hanging out with Jack? It's my pleasure," he said heartily; he did not make eye contact with her. "We're going to have some fun tonight, aren't we, pal?"

Jack nodded eagerly. "Let's start."

"After your mom leaves," Luke said. Then he leaned closer and whispered, "We don't want to make her jealous, right?" Then he turned to Crystal and said, in an almost accusatory tone, "So when's he picking you up?"

She blinked at the bleakness in his voice. She had to be imagining it. "I'm, uh, meeting him downstairs, actually."

A storm cloud gathered on Luke's forehead. "He's not picking you up? What kind of guy doesn't pick a woman up for a date?" He turned to Jack. "A gentleman always comes to the door. Remember that."

Crystal sucked in a deep breath. "*I* told him to meet me there. It's just… I don't know—easier." In truth, the thought of having Jed in her *home* this soon was too much. Too intimate. Too fast. She glanced at the clock. "I'd better go down."

Luke didn't respond, but Jack hollered, "Have fun, Mom." And then, he turned his attention to the bags as Luke began pulling items out and explaining what he had in mind.

It was a wonderful scene, and suddenly, she was loathe to leave. She didn't want to be on the outside looking in. She wanted to be a part of this. She—

Luke paused to glance at her, hovering there by the door, but all he said was, "You're going to be late."

Clearly neither of them needed her. They probably didn't want her around. It was male bonding, after all. "Okay. You know where I'll be if anything comes up."

"Mmm-hmm." And this time, Luke didn't even look at her.

All right. She knew how to take a hint. With a sigh, she pulled on her coat, let herself out of the apartment and, with one last, longing look back, closed the door. It was stupid to feel left out. It was crazy to dread having dinner with a handsome man, someone most women of child-bearing age would kill to be dating. Jed wanted her. He made no bones about it. Luke, apparently, didn't. So she'd toss back her head and put on a smile and enjoy this date. Even if it killed her.

When she came into the restaurant from the back, through the kitchen, as she usually did when she came from home, Chase was there to greet her at the door. "Crystal!" He took her coat and looked her up and down. "You look fantastic."

"Thanks."

"Come on. Jed's already here."

So early? She swallowed her sudden nervousness as she followed Chase into the restaurant. How long had it been since she'd been on a first date? She couldn't remember because her last first date had been with Brandon. Had it been junior prom?

Jed stood when he saw her. Dressed in a clean white shirt, dark jeans and a blazer, he could have stepped right off a magazine cover. But that wasn't all. As he smiled at her, he whipped out an enormous bouquet of roses from behind his back and presented them with a bow. "My lady."

Oh, dear. She stared at him, speechless. If he had planned to sweep her off her feet, he'd certainly started off right. It was wrong for her to wish she was still upstairs with Luke. Wasn't it?

"Jed, you shouldn't have," she said as he pulled her chair out for her.

"You deserve a nice evening out. Don't you?" he said as he held her seat.

Well, he certainly had that right. Maybe Roni and Lizzie were right, too. Maybe she needed to give this handsome, charming man a chance. One date—and not a date spent mooning over a man she couldn't have. She should focus on *this* man. She owed him that much.

Once she made the decision, once she relaxed, she did have fun. Jed was amusing and engaging and kept her laughing. And then, after dinner, he held her coat for her, which, while not entirely necessary, was very chivalrous. The he took her hand and they stepped out the front door into the cool evening breeze. His ungloved hand was warm against hers. They walked around the building toward her place, but as they turned the corner, Jed let go of her hand and put his arm around her shoulders. "So," he said. "Did you have a nice time?"

She couldn't lie. "It was wonderful. Thank you."

He pulled her closer, and she let him.

Give him a chance. Give him a chance.

It was a pleasant walk around the building to the stairs of her apartment. In unspoken accord, they stopped at the bottom of the steps and he took her in his arms. Her stomach did a somersault. He was going to kiss her. She knew it—

She barely had time to take a breath before his lips came down on hers.

Give him a chance. Give him a chance.

It was a gentle kiss, a questing kiss, a *nice kiss*. But that was it. There was no sharp thrill, no mind-numbing excitement, no breathless insanity.

When he lifted his head and their eyes met, he sighed. "You don't feel it, do you?"

She couldn't give him anything but the truth. "I'm sorry."

He buried his face in her shoulder and laughed. "Please. Anything but that."

She grimaced at the wryness in his tone. "I'm—" She cut herself off in time. "It was a lovely evening. Thank you for everything. I had a really great time."

He nodded. "Thank you. For finally giving me a shot. I appreciate it."

She tipped up her head and smiled. "Thank you for making me feel wanted. It was nice."

"Damn," he said as he stepped back. And when she arched an eyebrow, he responded, "It's a damn shame. We would have been great together."

Yeah. If only his kiss had moved her, even a little bit.

Crystal walked through the door with an armful of roses, a smile on her face and smudged lipstick. Luke's heart dropped. Surely he hadn't secretly hoped the date would be a disaster. Had he?

Well, now he knew. And damn. It hurt. It hurt a lot. So much it was hard to breathe. He was an idiot to have turned her away and now he would lose her because of it. If he hadn't lost her already. He should have just taken her to bed when he'd had the chance.

Her eyes widened as she glanced around the kitchen, and he suddenly realized that he and Jack had completely forgotten to clean up. An assortment of cooking and baking utensils were strewn over the counters, and various ingredients speckled every surface. "Um, we were just starting to tidy up," he said quickly.

"Hmm." She opened the counter under the sink and pulled out a vase, filled it with water and shoved the rose stems in. Then she shouldered off her coat and draped it on a chair.

"Did you have a nice time?" he asked, grabbing a rag and pretending to wipe things.

"Yes." She smiled again. *Damn it.* "It was very pleas—" She froze and narrowed her eyes. "What is that on the cat?"

Jack yelped and he ran to scoop up Snickers. "Just a little lava. I'll go wash it off."

Lava? She shot a glance at Luke.

He batted his lashes. "We made a volcano."

"Ah. And what's this here on the table? It looks like a purple sponge."

He leaned in. "That is microwaved cake."

"Really?" Her nose kind of turned up, though it was clear she was at least pretending to be astonished by their feats.

"Try it." He broke off a pinch of it and held it up for her to taste. As her mouth closed on it, his finger brushed her lower lip, and she flinched. Then, he did, too. It was the jolt of electricity that did it for him. He had no idea what it was for her.

She looked away as she chewed and he stepped back; he'd realized he'd come too close.

From the bathroom, the cat yowled.

"Mmm. It's good," she said, her eyes widening.

"Why do you sound surprised?"

She smiled, barely met his gaze. "Because it looks like a sponge?"

Before he could respond—thank God, because he might have leaned in and kissed her or something equally crazy—a wet cat shot through the room with an offended wail. Jack followed with a towel in his hand. "Got it," he said triumphantly. "At least, I think I got it."

"Thank you, Jack," she said, almost stiffly, as though she had come close enough to feel Luke's heat, and then drawn back, singed. "Did you have a good time?"

Neither of them probably expected Jack's response, which was a loud, boisterous recounting of everything that had happened in this room since she left, including a detailed recital of each and every experiment they'd done and a fairly accurate accounting of the results. Although, Luke noticed, he did leave out the part about the unfortunate explosion and the incident with the cat. Which was probably prudent.

By the time Jack ran out of steam, they were both in stitches. It felt good, laughing with her. Hell, everything felt good with her.

Too bad it was probably too late to tell her how good it felt to be with her. Just be.

She caught his gaze and stilled. "Luke?" she said softly. "Are you okay?"

He tried for a smile. "Yeah. Oh, yeah. I just…need to get this all cleaned up." He headed for the sink.

She stopped him. "You don't have to do that. Not after—"

"A man always cleans up his own mess." Jack

piped up to parrot the mantra Luke had repeated but not lived up to tonight.

Crystal froze, then glanced down at her son, stunned. "How…? Where…? Where did you hear that?"

Jack thrust a thumb at Luke, who nodded.

"Yup. If we make a mess, we gotta clean it up. Them's the rules," Luke said. And in his estimation, if everyone followed such rules, the world would be a better place.

Crystal stared at him for a second and then threw up her hands. "Well, if you think I'm going to argue with that, you're crazy." And then, with a laugh, she headed for her bedroom. Most probably to change. He tried not to think about it.

By the time she emerged, wearing yoga pants and a Cougars sweatshirt, he and Jack were done cleaning, even though the poor kid was really dragging butt. It had been a pretty long evening. When he yawned, Crystal laughed and ruffled his hair. "Way past your bedtime, young man," she said.

"Aww." He shot a pleading glance at Luke.

He snorted a laugh. "Don't look at me. I'm not the boss."

"Mom! Please?"

She ruffled his hair again and then pulled him in to kiss the top of his head. "Time for bed," she said firmly. "Tell Luke thank you and then go brush."

The kid shot him a conspiratorial look and a thumbs-up. "Thanks, Luke. It was a blast."

"Sure thing," he said. Still, it took a couple more nudges before he finally got into bed.

As she closed Jack's door, Crystal sighed heavily, and Luke realized that he was outstaying his welcome. He should probably go home, though his stark little house didn't seem so homey at the moment. But before he could plead fatigue and excuse himself, she turned to him and said, "Do you want some tea?"

There was nothing on earth he wanted less at this moment than *tea*, with the possible exception of a root canal, but he said yes. He was really saying yes to more time with her.

They sat across from each other at the table in her spotless kitchen and waited for the water to boil. Luke took the lead, just because he hated the silence. "So," he said. "Did you have a good time?"

When she looked at him, the faux enthusiasm she'd shown earlier was gone. She shrugged. "It was nice. I mean, he was nice. Everything was…nice."

His heart lifted. "Just nice?" Was it wrong to prod?

"No, it was very nice. He went way out of his way to make sure I had a good time."

"And?"

She shrugged again. "And I had a good time."

The silence fell again and Luke fiddled with the

salt and pepper shakers formed, for some reason, like ladybugs. "He kissed you."

When she didn't respond, he glanced at her. Her brow wrinkled. "You and I are just friends, Luke," she reminded him.

He ignored the reminder. "Did you like it when he kissed you?" Why was he punishing himself? Why? Oh, he knew why, damn it. He couldn't have her, but he still wanted her to want him. Hope was a like greased pig sometimes. But still, he tried to grab it.

She didn't respond. He hadn't expected her to. Regardless, he pushed on. "Did you like his kiss better than mine?" Yeah, he knew he was acting like a gawky, besotted high-school dork, but he needed to know. This, he needed to know. So he looked straight at her. He was surprised to see tears in her eyes. "Did you?"

A fat drop slipped and made a track down her cheek. "No." So soft, he almost missed it.

But he didn't. He didn't stop his grin, either. She'd liked his kiss better than Jed's. She'd *said it*. Out loud.

He didn't understand why she responded with a frown. "What?" he said. Sometimes women were too mysterious and a guy just had to ask.

"What?" she retorted, which wasn't an answer.

"Why are you frowning?"

"Why are you grinning?"

"Because you said you liked my kiss better." *Duh.*

Her frown deepened. "Why do you care? You don't even *like* me."

What? "I like you!"

She made a face. "*That way.* You don't like me *that* way. You know what I mean. 'Let's be friends,'" she said, imitating his deep voice. Then she made quote marks and added, "'I just wanna be friends.' You had your chance, dude. You made your feelings clear."

"No. I didn't say I didn't like you…that way," he sputtered. "I said that Brandon was why—"

She silenced him with a sharp look. "I loved my husband, Luke, but Brandon is dead. Aside from that, you knew Brandon well enough to know…he wouldn't have wanted me to be alone forever. He wouldn't have wanted Jack to grow up without a dad."

Luke stared at her as those words sunk into his brain. He couldn't argue the point. Brandon *would* have wanted that.

But then, he hadn't really been thinking about what Brandon wanted, had he? He'd been too obsessed with what he wanted, what he needed, what he'd thought was best. Hell, he hadn't even bothered to consider what *she* needed.

It wasn't fair to tell her they couldn't be together without telling her everything. Without opening up and revealing his darkest demon. But he couldn't do that. If she knew that, she'd never want to see him again. Could he survive that?

No. Not now. Not now that they'd become close.

Before he could form a response, she barreled on. "So let's just acknowledge that Brandon isn't the point of this conversation, is he?"

"He's...not?"

She sniffed. "You made it really clear that you were not interested in all this." She made a swishy hand gesture over her face and body.

"I am so!" he barked, before he thought about it. Probably why it came out like that. Like he was in third grade or something.

Her mouth closed with a snap. She sat back in her chair. Folded her arms. Shook her head.

Because she was silent for so long, he finally asked, "What?"

Her gaze sharpened. "You want me. I definitely want you. Why aren't we...together?" By the last word, her ire had deflated; it was a whispered remnant.

The teakettle shattered the moment, but to Luke, it was a reprieve. Not a long one, for sure. But long enough for him to get his thoughts together.

Crystal found herself caught between anger and sadness—and not for the first time—as she made their tea. It probably took longer than it should have, just because she needed time to work through all those jumbled feelings.

One thing was clear. She wasn't interested in Jed, or any other man alive. Luke was her guy. She knew this to the bottom of her heart. If she couldn't have him, she didn't want anyone. If he didn't want her, there were many more cats in her future.

Oh, she'd fight for him. Wrangle her way through whatever this was. No matter what, she wouldn't let him slip through her fingers without one hell of a fight. With a heavy sigh, she returned to the table, two steaming mugs in hand. She set one before him and then took her seat, opposite, so she could look into his face.

"Well?" she said when she decided he'd stirred his tea long enough, thank you very much.

He might have flinched. He definitely sucked in a lungful of air. As he breathed it out in a slow, measured release, he met her gaze. "This is difficult for me," he said softly.

She reached across the table and covered his hand with hers, but she didn't speak. This was a time for listening—she could feel it in her soul.

"I do want you. God." He raked back his hair. "You have no idea… And, yeah. I feel guilty. I can only hope Brandon would forgive me."

A laugh erupted from her throat. "Really? Do you think he wants me to be alone?"

"No!"

"Do you think he wants me with Jed Cage?"

"No." This was said a little more adamantly.

"I can't think of anyone he'd rather be a father to Jack than you. And frankly, I know he'd want you to be with me over anyone else. I know it."

"I suppose. But I can't help feeling like I'm being disloyal." He drew in a deep breath and then blew it out. "But, damn it, Crystal, when I learned you were going on a date with Jed… I was angry and jealous and frustrated. But the truth is, I was most angry with myself."

She quirked an eyebrow. "Why?"

"It goes way back. As a kid, I always felt 'less than.' And even though I'm past that, it still pops up every now and again."

"And?" she prompted when he paused for too long.

"I can't help thinking that you…deserve better that someone like me."

Better? She wanted to smack him. He was exactly what she wanted. Why couldn't he see that?

"Maybe a guy whose face doesn't frighten children?" He meant it as a joke, but she didn't laugh. "My scars are—"

"I think your scars are sexy."

He froze. Prickles danced up his spine. "What?"

"They're the sign of a survivor, Luke," she reminded him gently. "If you want to escape my clutches, you're going to have to do better than that."

When he didn't respond quickly enough—because, what the hell could he say?—she sighed. "Look, I understand why you pushed me away. But you didn't have to. You could have just told me what was really bothering you."

He let out a harsh laugh and raked his hair in a brusque, jerky motion. "Yeah. How could *that* go wrong?"

"Instead you let me think you weren't interested. Which one do you think hurt me more?"

His chin jerked up. He stared at her. "I would never hurt you. I mean, that wasn't my intention. I—"

"Stop." It was too painful to let him continue. "I'm not judging your decision. I understand why you did what you did."

"Really?" Finally, a hint of hope in a dismal expression.

"I just want you to understand how much I truly, deeply…care for you." She lifted a shoulder and huffed a laugh. "Scars and all. Literally." And, because it needed to be said, she added, "I want to *be* with you, Luke."

His brow furrowed. He shook his head. "Even if I might not be able to give you…you know, what you want—?"

She couldn't hold back her frown. "How the hell do you know what I want? Have you ever asked?"

"I… Ah…" He stared at her. "What…do you want?"

This time, she took both his hands in hers. "I want companionship. I want laughter. Love and affection. Relationships aren't just about sex, you know."

His eyes widened and his nostrils flared in a nearly comical reaction.

"Besides, I can take care of *those* needs myself if I have to," she said, tongue in cheek. For some reason, he looked gobsmacked. "What I can't do is cuddle with myself at nighttime when it's cold. Or have a fascinating conversation all alone—" She stopped short and then added, "Well, I *can* do that—and often do—but it's much better with a real person. Do you see what I mean?"

"I do." He nodded. His eyes were alight with a simmering…something. "I want those same things, Crystal."

By mutual, unspoken consent, they both stood and she walked into his arms. He wrapped himself around her, pulled her into the warm, fragrant cocoon of his embrace. He held her for a long time, and she held him.

"This is nice," she whispered into his neck, because it was.

He nodded. "I could get used to this."

She leaned back, so she could see his eyes. "Stay the night," she whispered.

Stay with me. Please.

Chapter Nine

Luke stared down at Crystal's face, shining up at him as it was. He couldn't deny her request because he needed it, too. He needed her touch. Her warmth. Her scent.

He lowered his head and touched her lips with his, gently, tentatively, and she allowed it. And, when the kiss developed into something sensual and glorious, involving nibbles and nips, she was the one who deepened it.

She was the one who broke away, too, but only to take his hand and lead him to her bedroom. He wasn't about to resist. Not with the hunger roiling in his soul. And not just hunger for sex. It was the spiritual hunger of one soul for its mate. The kind of togetherness that had no demands. No expectations. Simply…love.

But once they were alone, all of that spiritual hunger quickly devolved into a raging, pounding mind-bending lust. For the first time in a long while, he welcomed it. Gloried in it. Gloried in her.

"We have to be quiet," she whispered and he nodded, because he was supposed to. But, in fact, he was intently focused on her fingers toying with the hem of her dress.

When she slowly lifted off her black dress, revealing her creamy skin inch by mind-blowing inch, he stood there, like a statue, soaking it all in.

Beautiful Crystal with her hair loose and hanging down her back, the glow of welcome in her eyes. And—he swallowed heavily—the lacy black bra and matching panties that barely covered anything. He bit back a groan, pulled his woman into his arms and then, gently, laid her on the bed, eased down beside her and took her mouth.

Ah. She was, in a word, delicious. Sweet and warm and willing.

When he nibbled and kissed his way down her neck, she sighed softly and ran her fingers through his hair. But then—when he continued downward, and found her prominent nipple through the lace of her bra, and he took it in his mouth and suckled—those fingers dug in, scoring his scalp with her desire. That sweet pain, proof of her passion, aroused him even more.

Though he wanted to continue his exploration of her magnificent breasts—and they were magnificent: plump and round and a perfect fit for his palm—he continued his journey downward.

The feel of her skin, the taste of her, dazzled him. His pulse pinged in his temples...and elsewhere, but he was determined to be patient, to make her feel good, to make sure she understood just how badly he wanted her...and only her.

When she realized his intention, the true direction of his wanderings, she gasped. "Luke—" She broke off with a strangled moan as he found what he was looking for—the warm, wet crux of her thighs.

He stroked her first with his thumb, over the fabric of her panties, slowly, tauntingly. Then he pressed a little deeper, caressing her with indolent circles, smiling to himself when this made her moan.

Slowly, his fingers found their way beneath the elastic, and—holding her rapt gaze—he eased her underwear down. Because he wanted to see her reaction, he didn't look as he touched her, skin-to-skin. As he unerringly found that tender bud.

Her eyes closed. She threw back her head, arched her back and whimpered. "Please," she said, or something like it.

God, she was beautiful.

All he wanted, in that moment, was to give her

more. So he did. He opened her with his thumbs, and stared at the core of her femininity. But not for long. No. Because he wanted...to taste her.

And, ah. She was divine, glorious, like a warm summer day or a spring rain. He couldn't get enough and, judging from the way she locked her legs around his head and urged him on, neither could she. He could tell, from the way her body tautened, that she was close, but he wasn't finished yet. He still had more to share.

He worked her mercilessly, tormenting her nipples with one hand, filling her with the other and gently circling her nub with his thumb. And he watched her, adjusting his movements to match, to enflame her reactions. He delighted in every moan, every sigh, every guttural command.

He knew when she came. He felt it inside her. Then, when she collapsed, when she flopped onto the pillows like a wet noodle, he slithered up to the head of the bed and pulled her into his arms.

She cuddled into him. "Mmm" was all she said.

He took this as a compliment, given how sated she appeared. Her eyes were heavy-lidded and her cheeks were rosy, her lips slightly parted. He'd always thought her beautiful, but never so as much as now.

"Are you okay?" he asked. She turned to him and his heart hiccupped when he saw the tears in her eyes. "Sweetheart," he said, thumbing them away. "Why are you crying?"

Her smile was radiant. "I'm not crying. I'm just happy." She cupped his face in her palms and pulled him in for a kiss. "God. That was amazing."

"Even though you can take care of these needs by yourself?" It was only fair to remind her.

She kissed him through a laugh. "You, Luke Stirling, are one hell of a lover."

Which was generous of her, really, considering the fact that he'd only just begun.

Something flared in his eyes, something wild and hungry. She ached to touch him, so she did. Slowly, she slid her hand down his flat belly and found him, hot and hard under his jeans. An unholy thrill danced through her as she stroked him—his eyes rolled back and he groaned.

"You're torturing me."

She frowned at him, but it was only a playful frown. Maybe. "You're torturing me."

He blinked. "What?"

No need to beat around the proverbial bush. "I want you in me. Take your clothes off."

She loved the way his nostrils flared, the way his body came to attention, the way he was so excited, she had to help him unbutton his shirt.

When he stood to drop his pants and briefs, she stared. Her mouth watered. Because he was so beautiful. And so hard. He shifted over her and settled between her legs. Then he met her gaze and whispered, "Are you ready?"

Was she ready? Her body wept for him. She responded by wrapping her legs around him and nudging him closer. Thank heaven he was good at taking a hint. Or maybe he was just as savagely driven as she was. The kiss of his hot flesh made her shudder. She opened wider. "Please."

And, ah. Yes. He eased in, slowly, tentatively, filling her with heat and pressure and glorious delight. She couldn't help closing on him—the sensation was too delicious not to. He groaned and dropped his head onto her shoulder, panting for a moment as he prepared for the onslaught. And then, without warning, he moved again, easing himself out.

It was agony. She tightened her legs around him in protest, but—thank God—he wasn't gone long, and when he entered her again, it was a forceful plunge, eased by the slickness of her body. This time, he went deeper. Touched her more deeply than she could bear.

Somehow, she bore it. And the next thrust and the next. She gloried in the feel of his hard body moving against her, scraping her nipples, caressing every nerve inside of her, stoking her desire… but she didn't want him to get carried away and injure himself.

Oh, all right, maybe she wanted to be in charge

for a while. When she pushed him back onto the bed, he allowed it, though there was surprise in his eyes.

"Let me," she said as she mounted him. Ah. Yes. He filled her so perfectly. She settled on him and took a selfish moment to explore his body from chest to belly, trailing her fingers over his biceps, his abs and those beautiful survivor scars. And then, she tightened on him. His eyes widened. "Are *you* ready?" she asked, just to be polite.

"Mmm-hmm."

He held her hips as she rode him, holding his breath and working against her and with her as they played out this magical symphony without any words. Her body tightened as bliss came closer and closer, filling her with heady anticipation of the coming climax. Somehow, he knew she was nearly there. He leaned up to suckle her nipples even as he reached down to stroke her nubbin. She was lost then. Gone. Tumbling in a magnificent madness.

It was then that he let go, then when he released himself, with a great gush of hot breath, and a tortured groan that vibrated through her.

She collapsed on him—she couldn't help it. She was boneless and utterly sated. He put his arms around her and rolled them both to their sides, never breaking eye contact with her. Never even looking away. He was with her, utterly and completely. And she loved him. Loved him so much, she couldn't form the words. How lovely that in that moment, she didn't have to.

It was cute, the way he grinned. Wonderful the way he cuddled up beside her and wrapped her in his arms, murmuring nonsense into her ear. It was also cute that a moment later, his snore rumbled through the room. Still, he held her, as though he couldn't bear to lose her. Still, he held her. All through the night.

When Crystal awoke the next morning, it was from a delicious dream of a warm, snug sanctuary. It only took a moment for her to realize that the sanctuary was Luke's embrace. One arm and one leg were flung casually over her, a comfortable weight. His snore resonated around her and his exhales teased her cheek. But it was the vision of his gorgeous face, slack with sleep, that beguiled her. His beautiful lips, that proud jut of a nose. The ashy half circles of his lashes on his cheeks. The crease of the pillow imprinted on his cheek.

She couldn't hold back a smile as memories of last night came back to her in a delicious rush. Oh, her body warmed even more as she played it through in her mind, blow by proverbial blow. He'd been so generous, giving her orgasm after orgasm, while he'd only had one. It made her feel a little guilty— greedy, too.

She vowed then and there to do whatever she

could to meet his needs with the same enthusiasm as he'd met hers. And he had been...stellar.

He opened his eyes and caught her staring at him, and then, when she grinned, he grinned back.

"Good morning," he said with a raspy voice. She loved his morning voice. And his morning beard, which she petted tenderly.

"Morning." She kissed him, just a quick peck, but he grabbed her and demanded more. Given her vow of five minutes ago, she was duty bound to respond. Also, he tasted good. Earthy and honest and...*him*. "We should probably get up," she murmured. Jack would be stirring. There was breakfast to be made... But Luke tightened his arms around her.

"I don't wanna."

She chuckled at his little-boy voice. "Neither do I, but if we don't, my son is going to burst in at any minute and—I don't know about you but—I'd prefer to have clothes on when that happens."

"Oh, damn." He was out of the bed in a flash, which was a shame, because it had been so sweet, there in his arms.

She followed suit, though, and picked through the remnants on the floor for her own clothes. When they were both dressed, she followed him out the door, and then, because she couldn't stop herself, she swatted him on the butt. He glowered at her over his shoulder, but she could tell he was only playing.

She liked this side of him. She liked it a lot.

Jack didn't seem to be surprised that Luke was at the kitchen table for breakfast when he came out. Crystal knew she needed to address this because—if she had anything to say about it—Luke would be sleeping over a lot more often. Pity she had no idea what to say to her son about it.

Luke, however, went right at it. He paused in cutting his waffle, glanced at Jack and said, "Your mom and I are dating now."

To which her son nodded, and said, "Okay." And then added, "Please pass the syrup?"

And that was that. Stunning how easy it was. How easy he made it. But then, he made everything easy, just by being there.

After breakfast, Crystal headed over to Roni's to help her make baked goods for her wedding reception. Luke had taken Jack down to Pasco to pick out a Christmas tree and to show him the plane he kept in a hangar there, and she had the day off from work, so Crystal found herself with time on her hands. Perfect timing, because Roni needed a lot of help.

Lizzie and Sam were already there, up to their elbows in flour, as Roni schooled them on bread-kneading etiquette.

"You want in on this?" Sam asked, holding up her hands, clumped with wet dough as they were.

"Um, no thanks." Crystal made a face. "I'm happy to decorate or arrange cookies," she told Roni.

"Arrange cookies." Sam snorted. "In your mouth."

"Sounds good," Crystal retorted with a laugh. Sam was all bluff, but once you knew her, you had to love her.

They worked for a while, chit chatting about the wedding. Crystal was stunned to learn that Sam had agreed to be a surrogate for Mark and Roni, who wanted to have children and couldn't.

"Sam, that's incredibly generous of you," she had to say.

Sam, of course, shrugged. "Hey, he's my brother."

"She really is the best," Roni said, giving her sister-in-law-to-be a hug. Sam wasn't overly fond of hugs, but she tolerated it, which spoke to how much she loved Roni.

"Hey," Lizzie said, slapping her ball of dough for no apparent reason. "How was your date with Jed?"

Crystal froze. Good Lord. Had that been only *yesterday*? It felt as though a century had passed.

"Yeah. How'd it go?" Sam asked when she didn't answer quickly enough.

"It was nice," Crystal said, picking up a pad of doilies and placing them on the plates Roni had handed her.

"Just nice?" Sam and Lizzie asked in tandem.

"Yeah. He was a perfect gentleman and really went out of his way to make it fun. He's a great guy." Roni came by with a plate of Russian tea cakes, and Crystal snagged one. When she bit into it, powdered sugar went everywhere. "He gave me roses."

"Did he kiss you?" Roni asked.

Heat rose on Crystal's cheeks, giving them all her answer, although it was the memory of an entirely different kiss that made her hot. Still, their high-school *oooos* rose.

"But I need to tell you guys, I didn't…feel it."

Jaws dropped. Even Sam's.

"What?"

"But he's hot! How could you not feel it?"

Crystal shrugged. "To be honest—and I am being honest here—I've been having feelings for someone else. And Jed's kiss… Well, it confirmed everything."

"Someone else?" Roni blinked.

Lizzie gaped at her. "Who else is there? This is Butterscotch Ridge."

Sam stepped forward, her eyes wide and filled with certainty. "It's Luke, isn't it?"

Again, Crystal's blush gave her away. She didn't have to say anything.

Sam whooped and pulled Crystal into a big sticky hug. Sticky, because her hands were basically dough claws at the moment. But Crystal didn't mind, because Sam's approval, especially as Luke's sister, meant a lot to her.

As they kneaded and baked and chatted about how awesome Luke was and how perfect he and Crystal were together, and how much he needed a woman like her, Crystal…glowed. That was the only word she could think of to describe this uprising of happiness and peace. Here she was, surrounded by friends in a perfect world where she'd found a perfect man, and—and this part was important—there were cookies.

"I'm so happy for you," Lizzie said at one point. "But poor Jed." She thrust out her bottom lip; suddenly she looked just like Emma. "He lost a keeper." She sighed. "Roni is with Mark and you're with Luke. We're all practically family now." She found her glass and lifted it again. "To sisters," she said.

And who wouldn't toast to something as wonderful as that?

"To sisters."

For Luke, the next several weeks were near perfect. He spent every night with Crystal and most of the days with Jack, when he wasn't working at the ranch or helping out at the shelter. Funny, how well they fit together. How everything just…fit.

They attended Mark and Roni's wedding and celebrated Christmas together, the three of them, at the ranch with the rest of his family. It was more fun than any Christmas he ever remembered. And then, the week between Christmas and New Year's, they celebrated the birth of Emma's baby sister, Ella. Now, in late January, the winter weather had taken a momentary break from its moping, sending the sun out to dance over the frost-covered landscape. God, it was a beautiful day.

Luke paused for a minute, wiped his brow and looked up at the tree house he'd just finished, speckled by the sunshine filtering through the leaves of the old oak. Something swelled in his chest. It felt like happiness, a long-lost friend. And he welcomed it.

It wasn't just the pride of workmanship that warmed him so. It was…everything. How was it possible that his life had gone from being an empty shell to…this? This fullness? Just thinking about it, about her, about them, warmed his soul and caused an unbidden smile to curl his lips.

Crystal. Just her name gave him joy.

Yep. She was the reason for his lightness of heart. She'd opened her arms and her life to him. She'd given him the one thing he'd always craved. Absolute unconditional love.

Not to mention the fact that she let him make love to her.

And she liked it.

Oh, yeah. His grin widened.

She liked it a lot.

They made love nearly every night. Sometimes they just held each other and talked. She told him her secrets and he told her his. She was the only one, in fact, with whom he'd shared everything.

Well, almost everything.

She knew about his horror at waking up paralyzed. She knew about his struggle to stand, to take that first step, to learn how to walk again. She knew about those recurring nightmares he used to have, occasionally still had. She held him after those, and soothed him. She knew it all and loved him all the same. Mind-boggling. No one had ever loved him like this.

They agreed that, even though Brandon was gone, it was important to keep his memory alive, not just for Jack, but for themselves, too. Somehow, welcoming his friend into this, rather than struggling to shut him out, brought a kind of peace to his heart. A peace he thought he'd never feel again.

The thought of proposing to her crossed his mind—several times a day. When a guy found someone this perfect, it was smart to lock it down. But then, that ugly old guilt would invade.

Oh, Crystal was right. Brandon would have wanted both his wife and son to have a full life without him. He was just that kind of guy. He'd written home nearly every day when they were overseas. Granted, sometimes he had to send the letters in batches, but he wrote her every day. Talked about her, too. Bragged about his son.

Still, Luke couldn't banish the thought that Brandon was dead because of him…or the guilt that went with it. It was like a rain cloud following him around and threatening to unload at some inopportune time.

He wanted to talk to Crystal about it, but he was afraid to ruin what they had. And, if it hadn't occurred to her, he didn't want to bring it up.

That was an irrational thought, of course. He knew it was. But he just didn't know how to shake it.

Aside from that, this thing with Crystal was still new. They were both adjusting and learning each other's proclivities. For example, she really couldn't carry on much of a conversation until she'd had at least one cup of coffee in the morning, and he had a hard time remembering to *put down the seat*. And, of course, there was the toilet paper debate. He was an over and she—inexplicably—was an under.

It was only fair to give her some time to decide if this was what she wanted in a forever sense. It was only fair to give her a chance to change her mind if she wanted to.

With a sigh, he picked up the plans for the tree house and folded them up with a heady sense of accomplishment, and, if he was being honest, a hint of sadness, because he'd enjoyed working with Jack on this so much. Surely there was another project they could find? Maybe—

"Luke."

He stilled. His jaw tightened at the sound of his oldest brother's voice. He and DJ hadn't spent much time in each other's company since Luke had returned home, and for good reason. As Luke remembered it, they'd fought more often than not. It had seemed prudent to keep deep conversations at bay.

"DJ." Suddenly thirsty, he grabbed his water bottle and took a long drink.

"Can we talk?"

Damn. DJ's expression was stark. "Sure." Luke leaned against the tree and took another swig. "What's up?"

"Um, my office?" It might have been an invitation, or it might have been a command. Hard to tell.

"Fine." He tucked the plans under his arm and followed his brother into the house, girding his loins as he went.

DJ's office—formerly the old man's office—was not Luke's favorite place. It was akin to the woodshed of most kid's nightmares. How many times had he been called on the carpet in this dark mausoleum of a room? How many times had he been berated here? Belittled? Threatened? Beaten? More times than he could remember.

It made him feel small, just to be here, just to breathe in the air.

The desk was a monstrosity hewn of mahogany that dominated the west wall—the only wall with a window. It was set like that, with the window as a backdrop, so when the old man called you in to harangue you, he was surrounded with a halo of light that was blinding. The entire north wall—aside from the gloomy fireplace—was one enormous bookcase with volumes going up to the ceiling. Luke had always been intimidated by those books—books he could never have read back then. Now he felt a tingle of curiosity to explore the titles, just to see what the old man thought was worthy of gracing his domain. But this was not the time for that. Later. Maybe.

DJ sat behind the desk, just like the old man had, merely to remind everyone of his station. Of all of his siblings, DJ had been the most like the old man. Consequently, there had always been some gaping crevasse between them. One Luke had no idea how to bridge. And, frankly, he'd never had much of a desire to do so before. Now, the thought just made him sad. They were brothers. It would be nice to have a relationship.

It was clear DJ expected him to take a seat on the other side of the desk, but Luke responded to the feelings this space engendered in his heart, and rebelled. He remained standing. Set his hands on his hips, to underscore his independence.

"So?" he asked, trying to look bored so DJ would move this along.

His brother studied him—and his quiet insurgence—for a minute, then scrubbed his face with a palm and sighed. Yeah. If it was an intimate brotherly tête-à-tête DJ had in mind, it probably wasn't going to happen. Not today.

At long last he said, "A letter came for you." He handed Luke a battered envelope. "I mean, it came back."

Curiosity won out. Luke had to reach across the desk for it—which was annoying—but he did it. His gut tightened as he recognized his unit's address in Afghanistan, scrawled in the old man's handwriting.

"What's this?" he asked, fighting off the urge to thrust it back into DJ's hand like it was poisoned. Because it might be.

"It's a letter," DJ said dryly. "Looks like it's been around."

Indeed, several addresses had been scribbled over the first. One for his hospital in Germany, then Walter Reed, then the VA rehab facility. The final stamp read, Return to Sender. It had literally followed him around the world.

Luke stared at the thing and shook his head. "Why did he write me a letter?" The old man had never reached out. Sam had, lots of times, via email, mostly venting her spleen over something one of her brothers had done, haranguing him to come home, or updating him on the happenings in Butterscotch Ridge. Mostly the first two because, frankly, not much happened in good old BR. He'd had the occasional messages from DJ and birthday cards from Mark and Grandma, but never anything from the old man.

So why did he write this letter?

He'd asked the question rhetorically, and to himself, but DJ answered. Kind of. "I guess he had something to say," he said with a shrug.

"Yeah. I guess." Whatever it was, Luke didn't want to hear it. Not again. Not now. He shoved the letter into the back pocket of his jeans.

"Aren't you going to read it?"

No. "Later," he said, mostly to avoid the discussion. He nodded to the door. "I gotta go."

"One more thing," DJ said, before Luke could take a step. God, he even sounded like the old man with that commanding tone, so sure everyone would blindly fall into step if he so much as snapped his fingers.

"What?"

"So... You and Crystal are..." He swirled his hand.

Luke narrowed his eyes. This wasn't DJ's business. "Yeah."

His brother paused for a long while, and then asked, "You happy?"

Not what Luke expected, but he nodded. "Yeah."

And then, to his surprise. DJ stood and thrust out his hand. "Congrats."

Luke stared at that hand for longer than he should have, but it was purely because of complete and utter surprise. He took it then, and they shook. Like equals.

It was a strange sensation.

But he liked it.

"Hey, you." Crystal greeted Luke with a smile when she pushed into the apartment with an arm-load of groceries. He was sitting at the table with an open beer and some mail in front of him. "How's the tree house coming?"

Luke grunted and then, when she fixed him with a curious glance, he added, "Done. Except the final touches."

"Hmm." She set the bag on the counter and popped the milk and eggs into the fridge. Luke was usu-ally more animated when he talked about one of his projects. Hopefully his pain hadn't come back. She trusted him to tell her if it had; she trusted him to ask for help now, if he needed it. "Where's Jack?"

"He's at Roni's. She asked him to help at the bak-ery."

Crystal nodded as she finished putting away the groceries. "I'm glad the bakery is doing well. It's proof this town loves its carbs."

When he didn't respond to her attempt at a joke, she frowned. His attention was locked on the table. That muscle in his cheek flexed. Disquiet swelled within her. Something was wrong. She just knew it.

She sat next to him and took his hand, forcing him to meet her eye. "What is it?" she asked.

He nodded to the letter on the table. She tipped her head to read the—

Oh.

Oh, dear.

She tightened her hold on him. He'd shared a little with her about his relationship with his grandfather, enough for her to intuit there was plenty he'd left unsaid. "Are you going to open it?" she asked.

He frowned. "He hated me, you know. He hated that I was…not as smart as the others. And he didn't keep it a secret. He was a man to say exactly what he meant and he didn't care who he hurt."

She nodded. "Lots of people are like that when they get older."

"Yeah. Well, he was like that his whole life. And he thought, somehow he thought, that by yelling at me and reminding me what a loser I was, that I would snap out of it."

She rubbed his back. God, she wished she knew what to say, what to do, to comfort him. "Maybe because he thought you could…just snap out of it. He didn't understand that you couldn't."

Luke snorted. "No. He did not."

"It was his ignorance. Not yours."

He cupped her cheek in his palm, tried to smile. "That's a beautiful sentiment," he said. "It's utter bull, but a beautiful sentiment. Truth is, he was a mean old bastard."

She had to chuckle. "That, too. But if you look at it from his perspective, as difficult as it is, you can begin to understand why he did what he did—"

"I know why he did what he did. He was humiliated that I was defective, in his view at least. That the Stirling name was tainted. I mean, look at DJ, Sam and Mark. They're all perfect—"

"No one is perfect."

"And what was I in comparison?"

What was he in comparison? Seriously? Did he not see his own worth? His lack of faith in himself irritated her, which was probably why her tone hardened when she said, "Wow. I can't believe I'm hearing this from you."

He looked up from the letter to frown at her. "What?"

"The man who learned how to walk again? The man who pulled himself out of an emotional abyss? The man who has guided my son through his academic challenges, and made his life so much easier? So much better? Where is this whining coming from?"

His jaw dropped. He gaped at her. Then he sputtered, "I'm not whining."

"You kind of are. Yeah. Okay. Your grandfather was an ass. He made you feel like crap. And then, you found your own way. You found a path, and made a life for yourself. I'm not saying you have to justify what he did. But if you can understand it, it will be a lot easier to move on. To forgive."

Luke stared at her. "Forgive?" The word tasted… rusty.

"It's the only way you'll heal, Luke. Right now, you're wrapping yourself in so much bitterness by hating him. The only one you are poisoning is yourself."

He frowned at her. "I don't hate him." He didn't. Did he? No. He hated the way the old man had treated him. It made him angry even now. But there was a fine line between anger and hate. Sometimes it was hard to tell the difference. "He was like a father to me. Until…"

"Until you started school?"

God, she understood him. She was the only one who did. "How did you guess?"

"Brandon went through the same thing, only it was his mother who made him feel like a lesser soul." Luke nodded. He remembered those stories. At the time, they'd decided that's the way "family" was.

Now that he was a grown man, he could see things in a different light. He could see he'd allowed his resentment to bleed over into his relationships with his siblings. Heck, they'd just been kids back then, too. They hadn't "been against him," even though as a boy, he'd been so certain the whole family only saw his failures.

But Mark had never sided with the old man. He'd even helped Luke hide when the old man came after him in a rage, as though he could beat the bad grades out of him. And DJ? He'd never stood up to the old man, but he'd definitely tried to calm him down more than once, distract him when he was in a rage at Luke. Sam was the only one who could get away with blatant insurrection. The old man tended to treat her differently, because she was a girl. He'd laugh when she tried to defend her brother. And then he'd laugh harder when she was enraged by his patronizing tone.

Somehow, Luke had rolled them all up into the same bundle with the old man. In his mind, everyone had focused on his shortcomings. Everyone had laughed about him behind his back…and not just his siblings. Everyone in the entire town. The feeling that he didn't fit in at home had become a filter that had distorted his view of life.

That chip he'd carried on his shoulder for so damn long? It had been his own conviction that the world, and all its inhabitants, would reject him if he gave them a chance.

And his solution? He never gave anyone a chance.

The people who had eventually entered his bubble had crashed their way in. The way Crystal had.

"So?" she said, yanking him back to the moment. "Are you going to read it?"

He fingered one edge of the envelope. "I... I don't know."

"Do you want me to read it first?"

God, no! Though he appreciated her offer, when he thought of the hideous screed that letter could contain, it horrified him. He couldn't bear the thought of her reading what the old man really thought of him. He knew, logically, it wouldn't change the way she felt about him, but he simply didn't have the courage. "It's okay. I'll read it." He picked up the letter and shoved it back into his pocket. "Later."

She smiled at him, kissed his forehead, rubbed the knot in his neck and, generally, made him feel good again. "You read it when you're ready. If you need me, I'm here. Okay?"

"Yeah."

"Now, what do you say we head over to the bakery, find Jack and see if there are any goodies left?"

Which, frankly, sounded like a very good idea.

Chapter Ten

Luke was able to ignore the presence of the letter for most of the rest of the day, but as he was lying in bed that night, with Crystal curled up beside him, he couldn't put it out of his mind. It called to him.

Finally, the conflict annoyed him enough that he carefully untangled himself from his warm nest, pulled on his jeans, boots and a sweatshirt, grabbed the letter and padded outside. He kicked aside a small tuft of snow, sat down at the top of the stairs and drew the cold night air into his lungs. It was a dark, quiet night. No moon shone through the clouds but there was enough light from the streetlight on the corner to read.

Still, it took him a moment to rip open the envelope, and a moment more to pull the letter out. Unfolding it was harder.

Even though he knew who wrote the damn thing, it was still a shock to see his name, in the old man's scrawl, at the top. He'd had a particular brand of chicken scratch, the old man, one that matched his ornery and difficult personality to a tee.

It took a couple more deep breaths before Luke could focus his attention on the body of the letter and work out what it said. As he read, he heard the old man's voice in his head.

But then, didn't he always?

Luke,

It's clear by now that you're not coming home, but I have some things to say to you, and I don't know how much time I have left. The old ticker is acting up and Doc Weaver says I should get my affairs in order. This ain't ideal. I'd rather have this talk face-to-face, but the fact is, you're as mule-stubborn as I am.

When I think about the last time we spoke— right before you stormed out the door—I feel only regret. It would have been different if I'd known it would be the last time I'd ever see you. I would do anything to take back what I said, but life don't work that way.

I know I was tough on you growing up. Tougher on you that I was on the others. But

*it was only because I saw so much of myself in
you, Luke. And I wanted better for you.*

*I'm a crusty old bastard and I know it. And
I've made mistakes in my life. I ain't gonna
deny it. But one thing is true. I love you, son,
and I always have.*

*Please forgive me, if you can. I only ever
wanted the best for you.*
Your Grandfather,
Daniel Stirling, Sr.

It was dated a few weeks before he died.

Luke stared at it for a long time after, though he
saw nothing...except memories. The old man's rage.
His rants. The lectures...

But suddenly, he also saw images of other times.
Times he might have pushed to the back of his mind.
The times that had become too painful for that boy
to recall. The endless hours they spent fishing together when Luke was young. The talks. The way
the old man comforted him when Dad died...

It hadn't all been bad, had it? That didn't negate
the abuse. It most certainly did not. But it helped,
a little, to understand that his grandfather hadn't
acted out of disgust. Or hate. He'd just been an old
man unsure how to deal with a troubled kid. Could
he forgive that?

Well, he didn't know—but he could definitely
work on it. He'd loved the old man once, which was

why his inability to please had hit so hard. Knowing that his grandfather had loved him, too, helped. Really helped.

He tipped his face to the sky, and released the bitterness he'd carried in his heart for so long. He let all the bad feelings go, clung to the good ones. He didn't need the darkness in his life anymore. He really didn't.

It wasn't until he folded the letter back up that he noticed a postscript on the other side. Just one line, but it hit him like a tidal wave. It filled his heart and soul with a peace unlike anything he'd ever known.

It was the one thing he'd always wanted to hear. The only thing that had mattered to him for so long. Right there, on the back of the letter. One short sentence.

I'm so proud of you, son.

As he stared at those words, a fat raindrop splatted on the paper. It had to be a raindrop, didn't it? Even though it wasn't raining?

But, damn, that was beautiful.

And, damn, he was glad he hadn't burned the letter.

Luke was different in the morning. Crystal couldn't put her finger on anything specific, but she *felt* it. When she opened her eyes, it was to find his head on the pillow next to hers, his eyes wide and clear and trained on her.

"Good morning," he said, and when he smiled, there were no lingering shadows.

"You read the letter." Somehow, she just knew.

His grin widened, his eyes teared up, but he sniffed and swiped at his eyes in a manly manner. "Yeah."

"I'm glad."

"Me, too." He edged forward and kissed her. It was a slow, sweet salutation.

She cupped his cheek and kissed him again. At long last, and because nothing else needed to be said—at least not this early in the morning—she murmured, "Mmm. I don't want to get up."

He chuckled. "Let's stay in bed."

"That sounds pretty good." They cuddled closer. His hand eased over her nightie, heading for blissful realms…

But then, only a second later, Jack hollered, "Mom! We're out of milk!"

They both laughed, but Luke was the one to kick off the blankets and pull on his shorts. Crystal cuddled back down into the warm bed, covered her head and ignored the noises coming from the kitchen. But, about a half hour later, when the smell of bacon wafted into the bedroom, she had to get up. Who wouldn't?

She padded into the kitchen in her robe with her

nose in the air. "Hey!" she squawked as the first thing she saw was Jack feeding bacon—precious bacon!—to the cat. "Don't do that."

"She likes it, Mom."

Crystal snatched the bacon from his hand. "It's too salty for her."

"Mom!"

She sighed and crossed her arms. "Go google it." She handed him her phone and waited as he tapped in the question. When his face fell, she knew he'd found it. She rubbed his back and murmured, "Sorry, hon." She turned her attention to Luke, who had, apparently, destroyed her kitchen once again. There was batter everywhere. How on earth had he splattered some on the window?

Fortunately, her arms were already crossed, so she didn't have to go to the trouble of doing it again. "And what are you doing?" she asked Luke's back.

He turned around, revealing her long-suffering waffle iron. "I was making you breakfast in bed."

Jack snorted. "But you went and ruined it by getting up."

"Well, ex-squeeze me," she said, then moved the bacon plate away from the cat, who was, apparently, stalking it.

"It's almost ready," Luke announced as he set her coffee right in front of her.

"Mmm," she said as she cupped her palms around

the mug and drew in the earthy scent of freshly ground beans. "My precious."

"Jack, come help me, would you?" Luke called.

Crystal relaxed into her caffeine fix as she watched her two boys fill three plates with scrambled eggs and disfigured waffles, and bring them to the table. It was a lovely, domesticated scene, one that filled her heart with joy. "You are too kind, sir," she said when Jack set her plate before her. He just snorted a laugh, and took his place at the table.

"So," Crystal asked Jack as they all started eating. "What shall we do for your birthday?" It was coming up, in a couple weeks.

He made a face and poked his waffle. "I dunno."

"How about a party?"

Wow. That went over like a lead balloon, judging from Jack's expression.

Still, Crystal pressed on. "Don't you want a party?"

"Mom," he said, rolling his eyes. "No one's going to come."

"What do you mean, no one's going to come?"

He rolled his eyes again. Or maybe he never stopped. "I have, like, one friend in the entire world."

She smiled brightly "Then we'll invite him."

"He's not going to come, if none of the other boys come."

"Then he's not much of a friend, is he?"

Jack rolled his eyes.

"I have a thought," Luke offered.

"Do tell," Crystal said in a silly voice that made even Jack smile.

"What if we throw a party—just for family, and a few select friends—at the ranch? We can do hay rides and skating on the pond, and even snowboarding if we get fresh powder."

"Snowboarding?" Crystal gave him the side-eye.

He grinned at her. "It's perfectly safe. We've done it for years. I'm sure we still have all the boards…"

"Awesome!" Jack declared.

Crystal had a different response. It was like the side-eye…on steroids.

"I swear. It's perfectly safe."

"You keep saying that."

"Ask anyone." He set his hand over his heart, just to convince her how sincere he really was.

But Jack was the one who broke down her resistance. "I want that, Mom," he said with those big brown eyes, and, of course, she had to relent.

Silence fell, other than the clanking of knives and forks as they tucked in. The waffles were a little raw for Crystal's taste, but she didn't say anything, and merely ate the crunchy edges. The eggs, however, were perfect. The bacon was perfect as well. It was crispy, just the way she liked it.

About halfway through the meal, Luke paused and fixed her with his attention. His expression was so intense, she stopped eating as well. She set her hand over his. "What is it?" she asked. He didn't answer right away, so she prompted him. "Luke?"

He cleared his throat and glanced at Jack, then back at her. "I, ah…" he muttered. She didn't urge him on again. She simply sat there and waited until he was ready. "I really like this," he finally said, gesturing to the table, although she knew he meant more than just breakfast together.

"So do I," she said.

"I've been thinking… I'd like…more." He met her gaze. "I mean, if you do, too."

"I'd like more, too," she said, in nearly a whisper, but he heard. She saw it in his eyes.

Jack wrinkled his nose. "Then make more," he said, waving at the waffle iron.

Crystal chuckled and Luke laughed with her. He turned to Jack and cleared his throat again, because, apparently, he was going to have to start all over again. "I mean, I like us. As a…family." He said the word as though he was tasting it for the first time.

Jack blinked. Then he glanced at Crystal. "Yeah?"

"How do you feel about it? You know. Me not being your dad, but dating your mom. We've never really talked about it."

He shrugged. "I told you I wanted you to date my mom when that Jed guy asked her out."

Luke nodded, though there was still a trace of trepidation on his face, the hint of a flush on his neck. "So you'd be okay with it if I...well, if I—I dunno, hung around for a while?"

Jack took another bite of bacon, then answered with his mouth full. "I like having you around. It's like having a dad."

And, oh. Crystal loved it, the way Luke's face broke into an elated grin.

"I like having you around, too," she said. "You make excellent bacon."

The second Crystal left the table to get dressed, and the bedroom door closed behind her, Luke leaned over to Jack. "Did you mean what you said?" he asked.

Jack shrugged and ate the rest of his bacon. Then he grabbed another slice off the cat's plate. "Yeah."

"Okay." Luke sucked in a deep breath. "So how would you feel if... I asked your mom to...marry me?"

"You mean like a forever thing?"

"Yeah. A forever thing." He liked the way that tasted.

Jack stilled. "Would that make you my dad?"

Luke swallowed. Hard. "I'll never replace your dad." No one could replace Brandon. No one. "But I will be a dad to you, if you want one. Fair enough?"

Jack stared at him for a moment, then he nodded. "Yeah. I'd like that." And then, with no warning, the boy launched himself into Luke's arms and hugged him like he never wanted to let go.

Luke was walking on air as he headed into the ranch that afternoon. The woman of his dreams accepted him exactly as he was and he had her kid's permission to make it official.

He was so happy, he was almost leery, because in the past, he'd noticed that when good things happened, sometimes bad things followed to muck everything up. It took some effort, but he forced away that thought. Better to focus on the good, live in the moment rather than fear the future.

He had Jack's blessing and Crystal would probably say yes when he proposed. Who could ever have imagined such a thing? He wouldn't ever have to be alone again.

Danny called out to him from the front room as he as he hung his coat on a hook by the door. Luke skidded to a halt and backed up, poking his head around the doorjamb. He had to bite his tongue to keep from laughing out loud.

"What are you doing?" he asked his brother, who was sitting at a tiny table covered with tiny teacups. His companions included a fuzzy bear, a baby doll with a butchered haircut and a unicorn. The chair was so small his knees were up to his chest.

"Isn't it obvious?" Danny said with a grimace. "Tea party. Come and save me."

That did it. A chuckle popped out. "But you look like you're having so much fun," Luke said in a needling tone.

"Of course, he's having fun," Emma said, entering the room from the kitchen with a plate of cookies. "Hi, Uncle Luke." She gave him a big hug. Only a few of the cookies tumbled to the floor.

"Hey, Emma."

"Are you here to work?" Danny asked hopefully. "I bet we can find a fence to mend or something."

Luke chuckled again. "Nope. I was hoping to catch everyone at lunchtime." His siblings usually came in for the midday meal.

"No one has come for lunch yet," Emma said.

"Is that why you have cookies?" Danny asked. "No one to guard the pantry?"

In response, she pushed a cookie into Danny's mouth. "Here you go, Daddy," she said.

Danny sat there, mouth full and eyes wide, begging for help, but Luke just grinned. After all, he'd done his time on Emma's tea-party circuit. It was only fair to let his brother have some fun, too.

He waved at them and headed to the kitchen where the housekeeper, Maria, was cooking up something delicious. "Mmm," he said. "Smells fantastic."

She looked over her shoulder at him and smiled. "Luke. Good to see you. Are you staying for lunch?"

"Sure." He nodded, leaning in to take a whiff. "Chili?"

"My special recipe," she responded. Maria had worked for the family for years. Just recently her brother had moved over from Pasco to help Roni with the bakery, but honestly, if she wanted to, Maria could have been a chef herself. Her food was excellent.

She took pity on Luke and ladled out a bowl for him before anyone else showed up. It was delicious. He was still raving over the flavors dancing on his tongue when Sam and Mark trooped in, all dusty and dirty from the fields.

"Hey, you," Sam said as she plopped down at the long table. "What brings you to this neck of the woods?"

He grinned at her. "Maria's chili, of course."

"It would taste better if you'd spent the morning working with us," Mark joked.

"I'm taking some time off," he said. It wasn't as though they *needed* him, at any rate. They had a full crew. Luke drew in a deep breath as he felt the old irritations coming back to him—like weeds choking a garden—even though he'd felt totally at peace with himself and his relationship with his family last night. He'd thought he'd dealt with all the pain, successfully packed it away. Funny, wasn't it, how one word, one sentence, one interaction, could stir up all the dregs of the past?

Funny, wasn't it, how your family had you frozen in time? Luke would always be that lazy kid the old man hollered at, at least to them. He didn't want that. He didn't want to resent his siblings. He was really tired of ignoring his feelings around them, pretending to not care. It was time to address it. If only he knew how.

DJ pushed through the door just then and his gaze landed on Luke. Lingered. Then he nodded with a grunt and took a bowl of chili from Maria, who served the others as well, then Maria left to take a bowl to Grandma in her rooms.

Their older brother sat down at the table with a thud. "Having trouble with the baler," he said, apropos of nothing, except maybe avoiding a conversation with Luke. "Gonna have to call that electrician in Pasco, I guess."

"I can take a look at it," Luke said without thinking.

His siblings all turned to stare at him. "What?" DJ asked.

"I can take a look at it. I had some electrician training in the service." Why did they all seem so surprised? Oh, right. Because they'd never asked.

"Wow." Mark waggled his eyebrows. "The marines actually made you useful."

Maybe it was Mark's tone that made the bitterness swell. He really wasn't sure. Whatever it was,

Luke swallowed it down and frowned at his brother. "Quit," he said.

Mark blinked. His easy smile faded. "What?"

"Just quit."

"What did I do?"

"You were teasing him," Sam said.

"I was not." Mark glanced around the table. "I wasn't."

"It sounded like that to me," Sam said.

"Well, I didn't mean it that way."

Luke blew out a sigh. Yeah, this was it. This was the moment. "To be honest, I always felt like I was the butt of your jokes," he said as unemotionally as he could. He didn't want to spark a fight, but he needed to be heard. Now. Finally. He just hoped they were ready to listen. Really listen.

"What?" they all chorused. He knew them well enough to tell that they were genuinely shocked at his bald announcement.

Sam paled. "Not me."

Luke sent her a little smile. "You all made fun of me. You know, because of my dyslexia. You know you kind of did."

Her face tightened. Her throat worked. "I'm sorry." She reached out and took his hand. "I didn't realize…"

Mark shook his head and blinked, as though there was something in his eye. "I never meant it that way.

I swear, Luke. I'm your younger brother. I just meant it…you know. To be annoying."

"It won't happen again," added Sam, who somehow always knew what to say.

Luke nodded. "It's okay. We were just kids then. I understand. I'm past it. But I just want you to know how it made me feel so it doesn't happen again moving forward. Okay?" Damn, it felt good to get it all out in the open, like a boil that had been lanced.

DJ was the only one who said nothing. He sat there, at the head of the table, and watched in silence. Then he cleared his throat and said, "Did you read the letter?" The question hit Luke like a gust of wind he hadn't expected.

"What letter?" Sam asked.

Again, DJ remained silent, letting Luke speak for himself. "I got a letter from the old man—I guess it missed me in my travels. But, yeah. I read it." He sent DJ a rebellious glance.

"Are you…okay?"

Luke frowned. Not the question he'd expected from his brother, but one he appreciated. They both knew how that letter could have turned out. "Yes."

"Good."

Good? Luke eyed his brother again and his heart softened. Maybe a little. Maybe part of turning around the family dynamics was Luke letting go of his old expectations and prejudices, too.

Wouldn't be easy, but he vowed to work on it.

And on that note, he smiled. At DJ. On purpose. Funny how good it felt when his brother smiled back.

With Jack's birthday just around the corner, Luke decided he needed to get him a special present. Not because he was dating the kid's mom or anything like that. But because he wanted to. Besides, it was a great excuse to go into the Tri-Cities and shop for an engagement ring, without causing any suspicion.

Because Jack had been so fascinated with his Cessna, Luke decided to get him a remote-controlled plane he could fly in the field next to the church. He rationalized that it was, indeed, a very educational toy. He also got Jack a couple of his favorite lectures on DVD. There was one on western civilization that delved into interesting connections through history, one on physics and theories about the universe and, his favorite, the one about classical music. He couldn't wait to see Jack's reaction.

The whole family was excited about the party. Even more so when they woke up that morning to find a ton of snow had fallen overnight—a rare February dump. DJ scrounged up the old toboggans from when they were kids and had spent snowy days careening down the steep side of the hill. He even had the crew shovel two paths up the hill so no one would have to slog through the snow—one halfway up they'd deemed safer for the young kids, and one that went all the way to the top for the adults. Then the guys set up tables, chairs and heaters in the gazebo so there would be a comfortable place to warm up. Mark was so thrilled they were having a kids party—finally—he went out and rented several bouncy houses, including a bouncy slide that was two stories high…even though it was literally freezing, and even though Emma, Jack and Jack's friend, Taylor, would probably be the only kids there.

But Luke was wrong. Emma, Jack and Taylor were not the only kids who came. A lot more people attended than he'd expected. And they all brought their kids, who swarmed the back lawn, running from attraction to attraction like manic sugar-fueled alien lemurs. The adults, for the most part, gathered in the gazebo around the heaters, drinking mulled wine and spiked cocoa.

All that mattered to Luke was the smile on Jack's face. Funnily enough, he did have more than one friend in the whole wide world.

Because there were so many people at the party, Luke decided to wait until tonight, at the bonfire, to pop the question to Crystal. Bonfires were romantic. At least, he thought so.

After the cake and the presents—and after Jack had whispered to Luke that he liked *his* present the best—Luke eyed the hill. He'd been eyeing it all day. Now that most of the guests had gone, he decided to give it a try. He hadn't done it in years, since he was a kid; the thought scared him a little, but excited him, too.

Crystal was at long banquet table helping Maria, Sam and Lizzie tidy up—so she wouldn't try to stop him—and his brothers and Jack were building the bonfire. The sun slanted through the trees the way it did on a lazy February afternoon. It was a perfect time. The hill called to him.

It took him a while to make his way up, but only because the snow had been packed down by the horde and was a little slick. He was halfway up when he heard a faint cry.

"Wait. Wait for me!"

He turned and grinned at Emma, who was making her way up the hill behind him. He couldn't help it. She was so freaking adorable with her bunny hat and cheery red cheeks. The toboggan she towed was almost as big as she was. He waited until she caught up.

"I wanna do it, too, Uncle Luke," she said with a bright smile.

He glanced at the gazebo. Lizzie was not in sight. "Did your mom say it was okay?" he asked. Because Emma had been sick most of her life, Lizzie had a tendency to be very protective. The last thing Luke wanted to do was annoy Lizzie. Besides, this part of the slope was very steep.

Emma's smile widened and her cheeks flushed just a little more. "She didn't say I couldn't. Besides, everyone else got to go." When he didn't respond, she batted her eyelashes. His niece did know how to twist his arm. "I know you'll keep me safe." And that, with such a trusting expression. He caved.

"All right. You can sit between my legs."

This fomented a pout. "Can't I go by myself?"

"No." Not only no, but hell no. "This hill is for grown-ups. You come with me, or you have to go back down to the kid's slope. Understand?"

The lip came out, but she nodded.

"All right then." He settled his sled at the peak of the slope right on the path the other toboggans had cut, then helped her settle in between his legs. Then he showed her how pulling on the reins would turn the sled this way or that. "Are you ready?" he asked.

Her *yes* was a breathless gasp. Her little body shivered.

"Are you sure you want to do this, Emma?" he asked. She was so tiny, it almost seemed wrong.

But her response was to look at him over her shoulder and glower.

"All right. Hang on…" And he pushed off.

Though he'd sledded this hill a hundred times in his life, the initial drop still stole his breath. There was barely enough of it for him to issue a frosty laugh. Emma, however, squealed as they flew down the hill, picking up speed.

It had been so many years since Luke had soared down this hill, it didn't even occur to him that the topography might have changed, so he was stunned when they hit an unexpected hummock and became airborne.

Luke released his hold on the reins to pull Emma closer, to hold her tight. When they landed again in the packed hard snow, it was on Luke's butt and off the rutted track. He was the sled now, but he had no way to steer. All he knew was that he had to protect Emma as they hurtled down the hill in the wrong direction…toward the thicket of trees now directly in their path.

Emma, clueless to the peril, squealed in delight.

Dear God, he might have said, or he might have thought it, but there was definitely a prayer in his heart at that moment. The blood froze in his veins as he saw just where they were heading. Straight for the biggest, fattest trunk in the bunch.

His instincts kicked in. He tightened his hold on Emma and used the momentum fed by his weight to turn her away from this approaching doom. It was a fraction of a second before they hit, but it seemed like forever.

Luke's back slammed into the gnarled trunk with a blinding impact that jarred him to his teeth. He let out a noise, a whisper, maybe a wheeze, but it echoed in his head. It was his all in that moment, his everything, that breath. A blinding light flashed, then darkness and numbness, punctuated only by more pain as he rolled the last few feet to the bottom of the hill, where he lay, mute and motionless.

His mind was blank, completely vacant for some unknowable stretch of time. Could have been a second. Could have been an hour. He had no idea. He was aware of Emma, appearing before him, her hair dappled in sunshine, her sweet baby face pursed with concern. Her lips moved, but there was no sound other than that irritating buzz.

She continued to call to him, though, and patted his face with her mittened hand. Finally the buzzing eased enough for him to hear. "Uncle Luke. Uncle Luke."

"It's okay, baby," he tried to say and then, because she looked so concerned, he smiled at her, but it was probably a grimace.

Jack appeared in his line of sight. Luke tried to move. Pain shot through his spine from his butt to his neck, a pain so intense he nearly passed out. "Jack," he rasped.

"Luke?" The boy tried to help him sit, but it was too hard and he was too heavy.

"Jack." Damn, it was hard to push out the words. "Go find one of my brothers. Tell them to bring the backboard." DJ ran regular first-aid trainings at the ranch—he'd surely have it in hand within minutes, if not faster.

Jack nodded and sprinted away and Luke turned to smile at Emma again. "It's okay, sweetie," he said.

Her eyes were wide and brimming with tears. It was a heartrending sight. "Do you have a boo-boo?" she asked.

"Just a little one," he said through gritted teeth. "I'll be fine."

"Okay." She patted his knee. He watched, as though from far away, as her hand moved, and horror rose in his soul.

Because he didn't feel a thing.

Chapter Eleven

Crystal stared at the doctor as he pointed out various smudges on Luke's X-rays, but not a word penetrated her brain. She was far too worried and upset—horrified, perhaps—with that memory of Luke's pale, unresponsive face after Mark, Danny and DJ had brought him off the hill on the backboard.

He'd lost consciousness, they told her, when they'd transferred him onto the board, and he hadn't woken up. The guys put a cervical collar around his neck, to protect his C-spine while in transit. Getting him into the truck had been the worst part.

He'd remained unconscious all the way to the

closest hospital—in the Tri-Cities—nearly an hour. Crystal had been there by his side, in the back seat of DJ's crew cab, holding his limp hand and talking to him as though he could hear her. Everyone else had followed in other cars, but she and DJ got there first, probably because DJ sped most of the way.

The only reason the nurse let Crystal into the emergency ward with Luke was because DJ lied and said she was family, bless him. And he was such a comfort. Always knowing when she needed someone to take her hand, or slip her a tissue. She was really warming up to DJ. In fact, she liked him quite a lot.

Now, Luke was being monitored by the staff as Crystal and DJ sat in a smallish office, looking at Luke's X-rays and trying to understand how bad the damage was.

"It's hard to tell," the doctor now said, in response to a question DJ had asked. "There's a lot of past trauma, so it's hard to tell from these X-rays how bad the current damage is. I've called for neuro and orthopedic consults, but I'd like to do an MRI to get a closer look. In the meantime, we're going to keep him here overnight. Possibly longer, depending on what we find."

DJ nodded. "Of course."

"You're welcome to wait in the lounge," he added. "Our cafeteria has pretty good pie." He stood, indi-cating the interview was over, and she and DJ followed suit. DJ had the presence of mind to thrust out his hand.

"Thank you, Doctor."

"Yes. Thank you." Crystal felt like a zombie as she followed DJ out of the office and down the hall to the waiting room. He slowed then, and looped an arm around her shoulder. Her first instinct was to stiffen up, but then, she realized his presence was too comforting to do so.

As they stepped into the waiting area, the whole Stirling family was there. Jack ran to her. "Mom!" he said as he flung himself into her arms. There were dried tears on his cheeks, which made her heart ache. "Is he going to live?" he said on a sob.

"Yes, honey," she said, holding him close.

He pulled back and stared at her, tentative hope in his eyes. "Promise?"

She smiled and smoothed down his hair. "The doctor wants to keep him overnight, and do some more tests, but yes. He'll live."

Crystal let DJ fill in everyone on the details. She led Jack to a bank of chairs next to the vending machines and a television set mounted on the wall playing a news channel on mute. She sat with a thud. Emma came to her, crawled into her lap and hugged her as Jack sat beside her. She needed their warmth right now, so she held them both close. They were such a comfort, she didn't want them to leave, but as it got later and later, with no real news forthcoming, the family agreed to call it a night and head for home.

When Crystal refused to leave, Jack insisted on staying with her. It took a lot of effort to convince him to go back to the ranch with Lizzie. She would have let him stay, but there was no comfortable place to sleep. Finally, DJ stepped in and told him that that he'd be more help to Luke tomorrow if he was well rested tonight. Maybe it was his words or his authoritative tone, but it worked.

After everyone else had left—even DJ, though begrudgingly—the nurse came and led Crystal to Luke's room. She sat by his bedside and held his hand and prayed. Luke had to be okay. She needed him to be.

She couldn't bear to entertain any what-ifs.

If she lost him now, it would destroy her.

When Luke woke up the next morning, he was in a hospital room. He knew it immediately from the smell and the sound of beeping machines. He'd spent enough time in places like this for the realization to send a shard of fear through him. His brain was foggy and his muscles were heavy, so he knew they'd given him strong painkillers. But, as foggy as his mind was, he still remembered what had happened. He remembered guarding Emma and slamming into the tree. He remembered the teeth-jarring thud and blinding agony.

Emma! Oh, God. Let her be all right. Please, God.

And he also remembered…the numbness.

Horror curled through him. Slowly, he lifted his head and focused on his feet, desperately trying to move his big toe beneath the blanket. When he couldn't get it to budge, he collapsed onto the pillow and stared up at the speckled ceiling.

What if it had happened again? What if he'd damaged his spine and was paralyzed? Again?

What would that mean? Would Crystal still want him? How would he…?

"Good morning!" He jumped as her too-bright voice cut through his dismal thoughts; she pushed into the room with a Styrofoam cup in her hand and smiled at him. "You're awake!" She set the cup on the bedside table and kissed him.

"How's Emma?" he blurted.

She smoothed back the hair on his brow. Her smile soothed him. "Emma's fine. Not a single scratch. You saved her, you know."

He shook his head. "I should never have taken her down that hill."

"It's okay. She's okay." She surveyed him for a moment. "How do you feel?"

"Fuzzy," he tried to say, but it came out all garbled. Also, his mouth was too dry.

She seemed to understand, and handed him a plastic cup with a straw, and when he couldn't hold it himself without tremors, she angled the straw toward his mouth and held it for him. Nothing ever tasted as good as cool clear water. He smacked his lips and she chuckled.

"You gave us quite a scare." Her expression was far too chirpy, her smile deliberately wide.

Did she know? Had they told her? His heart gave a hard thump. "What…?" he asked. It was all he could manage.

"What happened?" Her brows furrowed. "Well, you decided, for some reason, to go down that damn hill—"

He waved his hand. He remembered all that. Then he gestured to his hips, willing her to understand. *What happened to me?*

Her expression clouded. His gut jerked.

"The doctors say everything looks fine. Nothing out of place—you know, other than the remnants of…your older injuries. You've bruised your tailbone again." The same one he'd bruised when he fell out of the tree. Yeah. He felt that dull ache radiating in his pelvic girdle, but it came from far away. "Are you in pain?"

He closed his eyes and focused on sensation, then shook his head. Other than that numb niggle…nothing.

"Good," she said, but she didn't understand. No feeling was *not* good.

What if he was paralyzed forever this time? The future he'd been starting to see with her and Jack was suddenly in peril. He couldn't do that to them. Saddle them with a man who couldn't even climb the stairs to their house. Unable to face the thought, he turned his head away.

It was a damn shame she was stubborn and empathetic and wouldn't let him run from her.

She came around to the other side of the bed and locked her gaze on his. "What is it?" she demanded, and when he tried to look away again, she wouldn't allow it. "Tell me," she said, holding his cheeks gently in her hands, holding him captive with her gaze.

He cleared his throat as he struggled to find the words. In the end, he pushed out the fragments of his greatest fear. "Can't feel…my feet."

Luke hated the way her expression changed. But she sucked in a deep breath and stubbornly jutted out her chin, the way Crystal always did. She straightened up, marched to the bottom of the bed, threw back the covers and drew a fingernail along the bottom of his foot.

He nearly went through the ceiling. He shot up in bed and hollered, "Ghaaa!" The sensation he felt with that one touch filled him with such gratitude that he could barely contain himself. Also, it tickled.

Crystal came to his side then, and took his hand. "Did you think you were paralyzed again?" she asked. And before he could answer, she hugged him, hard. "Oh, Luke. I'm so sorry."

"I couldn't wiggle my toe," he complained.

She kissed his forehead. "You've been lying in the same position all night. No wonder you're numb."

He tried wiggling his toe again; this time he made it move. Yup. Felt lots of prickles, too. But he could *feel* it. *Oh, thank God.*

She smiled at him. "It's asleep. See?"

"Yeah." He did see. And it was wonderful. He flopped back on the pillow and stared up at her. "You can't imagine what's been going through my mind."

She ticked her head to the side. "You must have been terrified."

"I was."

She squeezed his hand. "But you're going to be all right. The doctor said once the swelling goes down, everything will be fine."

"The swelling?"

"Hmm." She grinned at him. "He also recommends you stop falling on your tailbone, by the way."

Luke chuckled. "I'll try."

She hugged him and his heart swelled. His soul sang. Ah. Life was good. A man had to grab that happiness and keep it close.

And then, all of a sudden, in that moment, he knew. He just *knew* that *this* was the right time. This was the perfect time to propose.

When she pulled back from their hug, he took her hand. "Crystal Giles Stoker…" he began. But before he could get any other words out, his nice quiet hospital room exploded...with Stirlings. They showed up just in time to ruin his big moment. Awesome.

But one thing was clear. He was going to ask Crystal to do him the honor of marrying him. And he was going to do it soon.

The next time Luke woke up, Crystal wasn't there, but Jack was sitting in the chair by the bed reading a comic book. "Hey!" Luke said cheerfully. "What's up, kiddo?"

This earned a frown.

Luke shifted to the side, to face him better, but it hurt, so he had to crick his neck to look at him instead. "What's wrong, Jack?"

It took a while for the boy to give an answer, and when he did, it was an angry one. "I thought you were really hurt," he said. "I was worried."

"Sorry." And when Jack frowned at him, he continued, "I don't know what to say... I was really worried, too."

That sweet face, which looked so damn much like Brandon, puckered up. "How could you have gone down that hill? Knowing how dangerous it was?"

Seriously? He sounded like...a parent. "Wait," Luke said through a laugh. "*You* went down the hill. I saw you do it like, six times."

Jack glared at him. "It's not the same."

"How is it different?"

"You're old."

Ouch. "I'm not *that* old."

"You ended up in the hospital. And no one would tell me what was going on. It was awful."

Were those tears in the corners of his eyes? "Jack—"

"I already lost one dad. I don't want to lose another."

Oh. Okay.

Hell.

Luke nodded. Despite the pain of the swivel, he took the boy, who was now snuffling, into his arms and held him. "I really am sorry," he said into his hair as he held him close. Jack wrapped his arms around him and clung. "I won't do it again. I promise." It was a true promise, because Luke had no intention of going anywhere near that hideous hill ever again.

Jack peeped up. "Do you? Do you promise?"

"Scout's honor." He held up three fingers.

The boy narrowed his eyes. "Were you even a Boy Scout?"

"For a while." Luke batted his lashes. "They kicked me out when I set a shed on fire."

Jack stared at him. "Really?"

"Ask anyone. Swear to God. I used to get in so much trouble."

"I'll bet." It was an embarrassing confession, but Jack's grin was totally worth it.

Then he sobered. "Listen, Jack. I need to talk to you about something—"

"You proposed?"

Luke blinked. "I... What makes you think that?"

Jack shook his head. "Dude. It's just logic. You almost died—"

"I didn't almost die—"

"Old people do stuff like that when they almost die."

Did they? "No. I didn't propose. We were interrupted. But I'm going to. Are—are you still okay with that?"

He lifted a shoulder. "She likes you. A lot."

"I'm asking how *you* feel about it. Your opinion is important to me."

Jack flushed a little. "Of course I'm still okay with it. I think you're great too. But..."

"But?"

"You need to find a cool way to do it."

A cool way? "I was thinking about proposing at Sunday supper."

Jack rolled his eyes. "Boring."

Luke blinked. "All right. What did you have in mind?"

He perked up a little. "I got a bunch of ideas. Okay. How about this... You could rent a blimp."

"Ah..."

"You could shave 'marry me' on the side of a cow. You have lots of cows."

Luke barked a laugh.

"Or, of course, go for the old standard... Skywriting."

Skywriting?

"You have a plane. Do you know anyone who skywrites? Or, listen to this, we could have a flash mob dance down Main Street—"

"Uh, Jack, where did you get all these ideas?"

His grin was bright. "I researched it. On the internet."

Luke had to laugh. "Okay, dude. It's a deal. You and I are going to figure out a kickass way to propose to your mom."

"Okay. But it's gotta be something no one will ever forget."

"You got it."

If Jack wanted something unforgettable Luke would have to devise something spectacular.

No pressure. No pressure at all.

Crystal was so happy to bring Luke home. She was worried that the stairs to her place would be too much for him, but he insisted on making the climb and wouldn't hear any arguments.

She loved that about him, the fact that he was so determined. But at the same time, she worried that his stubbornness might overshadow his reason.

At least he continued to allow her to massage him regularly. Over the next few days, it was gratifying to watch his flexibility expand. He also seemed to be in less pain. He still had the occasional nightmare, but he let her soothe him then, too.

There had been a moment, back in the hospital, when he'd taken her hand and looked at her a certain way and said her full name. She'd been fairly certain that he'd been about to propose, but the family had interrupted, and since he still hadn't done so, she decided she'd been imagining things.

It was all right.

She wasn't in any hurry.

She certainly didn't want to pressure him.

What they had was wonderful. They were a family. No piece of paper was necessary.

It was silly to want him to say the words. Wasn't it?

And the fact that today was Valentine's Day—and he hadn't said a word about that—meant absolutely nothing. Didn't it? He probably wasn't even aware of the date. Men just weren't into such things and—

"Are you okay?"

Crystal nearly bit her tongue as she jerked out of her gloom to smile across the kitchen at Luke. He looked so handsome with his sleeves rolled up, making burgers.

There was just something sexy about a man cooking for a woman.

"I'm fine. Just thinking."

"About what?"

She decided to go for humor. "How many pickles I want on my burger."

"Hmm." He went to the fridge and pulled out a jar, opened it and decorated her burger with a generous pile of slices, and set it in front of her. "This should do."

"Mmm." She popped a slice into her mouth, savoring the tart brine as it danced on her tongue. "Maybe a few more?"

He laughed. "Still a pickle fiend, I see."

She loved the glint in his eye. The glint that said he remembered her pickle obsession—and teasing her about it. "Can't get enough."

He turned to Jack. "We used to call your mom Pickles, you know, because she ate a lot of pickles."

Jack chuckled. "She still does."

A clarification was necessary. "For the record, *you* are the one who called me Pickles."

His grin was wicked. "And you loved it."

"Hurry and eat, Mom," Jack said as Luke delivered the rest of the food and sat down at the table. "We have to get to the ranch by two."

Crystal popped a pickle slice into her mouth. "Why are we going to the ranch again?"

Jack and Luke exchanged a glance. "It's the family Valentine's Day party."

Really? "Since when does your family have a Valentine's Day party?"

"We do this year."

"It's at two, Mom. Come on. We can't be late."

She smiled at them both. "Fine. But I'm not rushing lunch. In case you haven't noticed…there's pickles!"

Once they finished lunch, they piled into Luke's truck and headed for the Valentine's Day shindig at Stirling Ranch. Luke seemed a little preoccupied during the drive. So did Jack, for that matter.

"Are you guys okay?" she asked as Luke parked next to Sam's car in the drive.

"Fine," they both chirped, so she dropped it. If they had something they wanted to talk about, they would.

Her first thought when she stepped into the front room of the big house was that cupid had exploded. There was red everywhere. Even a couple crepe paper hearts hanging from the overhead light. The coffee table was covered with Valentine cookies, cupcakes and Luke's favorite brownies.

"Wow," she said as she handed Luke her coat. "This looks fun."

"Happy Valentine's Day!" Emma said, running to give her a hug. She'd been standing over the goodies, drooling, so Crystal felt honored that Emma liked her enough to break away.

"Oh, hi there," Roni said, coming into the room with another platter.

Crystal gave her a hug. "This looks awesome. Great job."

Roni blinked. "Oh, I just made the goodies. I thought you guys did the decorations."

Before Crystal could respond, Lizzie and Sam came in carrying juice and champagne bottles. Danny followed, carrying baby Ella, and of course, Crystal had to go and cuddle her for a while. She smelled so sweet, like baby powder and innocence.

It wasn't long before DJ and Mark arrived with Luke's grandmother, Dorthea, and then the party really started.

Jack and Emma had made everyone Valentine's Day cards, which they handed out solemnly. Then Emma gave everyone a play-by-play of her first Valentine's Day at school, which had been very exciting because some of the valentines had come with candy.

There was a great deal of fun conversations, delicious food, laughter and camaraderie. It was wonderful.

At one point, Luke popped open a bottle of champagne and he and Sam poured glasses for the adults. When he handed one to Crystal he caught her eye. His expression caused a sizzle to slither down her spine. Her heart jerked. Suspicion rumbled.

No. *They* hadn't done the decorations, but maybe he had? Could he have coordinated this whole event for one reason? Her pulse thrummed.

"Excuse me, everyone," he said, gently tapping his crystal goblet with a knife. "I have something I would like to share." When everyone turned to look at him, he went red to the tips of his ears.

She knew what was coming. Of course she did, but that didn't dim the trill of excitement dancing through her. God, she loved him. So much.

Her heart skipped a beat when he pulled a ring out of his pocket and said, "Crystal Giles Stoker…"

A gasp rocked the room. Then, silence fell.

Crystal couldn't hold back a smile. "Yes, Luke Anthony Stirling?" Since they were doing the middle name thing and all.

It made him grin and, she hoped, helped ease his way. He cleared his throat. "Sweetheart, I love you more than I thought it was possible for a man to love a woman."

"Oh, Luke, darling. I love you, too!"

But he wasn't done. "You and Jack have changed my life so much for the better. There is nothing I want more than to spend the rest of it with you as my partner. Would you do me the honor of being my wife?"

For some reason she glanced at Jack. It was no mystery how Jack felt about Luke, but marriage was monumental and she hadn't talked about this with her son at all—

Oh. But he was grinning and motioning her to move things along.

"Yeah," Luke whispered. "This was all his idea."

Oh, God. Her heart swelled. Jack and Luke had planned all this together. It was…

"Are you going to answer him?" Emma asked curiously.

"Yes. Yes. I will. Of course." Her smile brightened even more as he slipped the ring on her finger. Ah, how she loved sparkly things. Especially this. "Oh, Luke. It's beautiful."

Then, he kissed her to the sound of everyone cheering.

Afterwards, they were so busy gazing into each other's eyes, they nearly missed Sam's announcement of her pregnancy, which was wonderful news for everyone, but especially for Mark and Roni.

Oh, it was too perfect.

What a wonderful family. And now, they would be hers… Officially! Jack was going to have cousins and aunts and uncles and a grandmother as well.

And she? She was going to have it all. Everything she'd ever wanted. And more.

Luke awoke in a terror—skin clammy, heart pounding, that old nightmare echoing in his brain. It took a moment, longer than it should have, for him to catch his breath and realize where he was. And know that he was safe.

"Hey. Are you okay?" Crystal's soft voice floated over him, around him. Soothed him.

"Sorry to wake you." Luke scrubbed his face with his hand. "Bad dream." Again.

She stroked his back, trying to soothe him. "It's okay. Everything's okay."

Was it?

"What did you dream about?"

Same thing. Same thing he always dreamed about. "That day. The explosion." He paused because the last word stuck like a thistle in his throat. "Brandon. I…"

Somehow, she sensed that this time, there was more—something dark that he needed to share. "What is it, sweetie? You can tell me."

He could. He should. She was his fiancé. She deserved to know it all. Especially now. Before she married him. Aside from that, he needed to tell her. He needed to be free of the weight he carried.

He could only pray that she wouldn't hate him for what he'd done.

It was so hard to look at her in that moment, but he did. He sucked in a deep fortifying breath and then said the words that had been burning a hole in his soul since the moment he saw her again. "It's my fault Brandon is dead, Crystal."

She stared at him through the moonlight. Shook her head. Her lips moved, but it took a while for her to get the words out. They didn't surprise him. "No it's not."

"It is—"

"Are you saying it was *your* IED?"

What? "No!" Of course not. No. "Because he followed me, you see. Even when we were kids, he followed me everywhere. Did anything I did. It only made sense that he'd follow me to the marines. I should have known. I should have talked him out of it. But I didn't. I wanted him to join. I wanted him to come with me. I should have talked him out of it, but I didn't."

"Are you serious?" She seemed furious. Why was she angry? "Have you *met* Brandon Stoker? He was probably the most stubborn man on the planet, once he'd made up his mind to do something. He made that decision on his own. He was a big boy. *He* decided to join the marines."

"You're missing the point."

"I don't think I am. You didn't kill him, Luke."

"Well, I sure as hell didn't save him."

"You're not being fair to yourself."

"How can you say that?"

"All right then. Going back to that moment. What could you have done to save him? Push him out of the way?"

"No. There wasn't time." It had happened in an instant. "But that's not the point."

"Quit babbling about the point."

He didn't. "The point is—I'm the one who got him to sign up."

"Bull. Brandon always wanted to join the marines, at least for as long as I can remember. His Gramps was a marine."

"But—"

She snorted. "No. It was always his plan. You are not allowed to blame yourself. If you'd been the one to die, would your family have blamed Brandon for your death?"

"Of course not—"

"Then I just can't see why you think it's all right to carry that burden. If Brandon were here, you know he'd say 'just get over it, dude.' You know he would."

Luke stared at her. Yep. Brandon would have said something exactly like that. He would also have been furious that Luke had used his death as an excuse to stop living. In fact, he could hear Brandon, there in his head, calling him out.

He blinked as Crystal's logic sliced through his guilt. He'd carried it for so long, that guilt, believed it for so long, it was hard to let go.

She turned him around, then pushed him down on the bed and kissed him. "I know it'll take time. But it'll get better."

"Yes," he said, wrapping his arm around her and pillowing her on his chest. Much better. Perfect, almost. "It will. Because of you." At least, he dared to hope.

Oh, he'd still have to deal with his aches and pains and the occasional memory or dream. But he wasn't alone working on those issues. Crystal was here with him. With Jack, they were building a family of their own.

And that made all the difference in the world.

Epilogue

The wedding was a small affair, just close family, and held in the sitting room of the Stirling Ranch house. Chase gave Crystal away, Emma was the flower girl and Jack was the best man. All dressed up in a Mini-Me tux, he looked more like Brandon than ever.

Due to popular demand, however, the reception was a big party, with all Luke and Crystal's friends and family attending.

Luke didn't mind the crowd, though. He was too damn happy that Crystal was his—from now until evermore—to give a damn that everyone and their uncle was traipsing through the house.

It had been a difficult decision to have his nuptials here, in the old man's place, but Crystal had held him close and reminded him that part of making peace with someone—or their ghost—was embracing them with your heart. And, yeah, as usual, she was right.

He lifted his glass to the old man and threw one back in his honor.

His chest warmed and peace filled his heart.

Damn, that felt good.

Funny, wasn't it? How much his life had changed since he ran into Crystal at the B&G? It had changed for the better. So much had changed for the better. It was hard to believe he'd fought it as hard as he had.

But now, here he was. A husband and father. It was more than he ever dreamed he could have. But he wasn't letting it go. Not ever.

"Hey, Luke!" Jack barreled into him, disrupting his moment of gratitude.

"Hey, Jack. Whatcha up to?"

"Have you seen my mom? Can you tell her I'm going to Uncle Mark's to play with the dogs?" Jack had really embraced the idea of having aunts and uncles. He was staying with the family while Luke and Crystal were on their honeymoon and he was as excited as all get out to spend time on the ranch.

"Sure. I'll tell her," he said to, well, Jack's north end going south, because he was already gone.

And speaking of his bride… Luke scanned the crowd, looking for that beautiful white dress, but couldn't see it. She wasn't by the dance floor the caterers had set up in the front room, or at the tables laden with food in the dining room. She wasn't even in the clutches of hens gossiping in the kitchen.

A sudden urge to find her, hold her, maybe kiss her, took him and he increased his pace as he searched for her. He nearly ran in to DJ as he turned the corner. "You seen Crystal?" he asked.

DJ tipped his head toward the hall. "She's with Sam, I think."

"Sam?"

"She's barfing."

Damn. "Again?"

DJ shrugged. "I guess."

Poor Sam. The pregnancy had hit her hard. She never complained, though. At least, never in Luke's hearing. After listening to Lizzie tell tales about her pregnancy with Emma—and her baby sister, Ella—it didn't sound like fun. It sounded like torture. And the least of it was the morning sickness—which wasn't always in the morning. And, yeah. As he paused by the bathroom, a retching sound rose. He tapped on the door. "You okay in there?" he called.

Dead silence, and then furtive whispers on the other side of the door.

"Sam? You all right?"

"I'm good," his sister called. There was more whispering, the rustle of skirts and then, the door opened. Sam grinned at him and then opened it wider, revealing someone else hunched over the toilet bowl. Someone in white.

His gut wrenched. "Crystal?" He rushed to her side. "Crystal, hon. Are you all right?"

"I'm fine," she said as he lifted her up.

He cocked his head and grinned at her. "Too much champagne?" Hardly the first time that had ever happened to a bride, he imagined, even though Crystal wasn't much of a drinker. But she shook her head.

"She hasn't had a drink," Sam said.

"No?" He glanced back at Crystal.

She smiled up at him, but it was a wobbly offering. "Truth is, I've been feeling kind of icky all day."

He frowned at her. "Why didn't you say something?"

"And what? Ruin the wedding?" He recognized that stubborn look.

"It's probably just nerves," Sam said. "You go back to the party, Luke. I'll keep you company, Crystal."

He reared back and gave his sister a look. "The hell. She's my wife." Damn, it felt good saying that.

Crystal smiled at that, but shook her head. "I'll be fine. I promise. It always goes away after I throw up."

Something in Luke's belly swirled. "Always?" he said roughly. "How long has this been happening?"

Crystal frowned at him. "Just a few days. It's nothing. Really."

"Nerves," Sam said again. "It'll be better now that the wedding's over. Now that everything's normal again."

But it wasn't. Crystal threw up the next morning and the morning after that. Luke tried to ignore the effect this had on their honeymoon—which consisted of a week at a B&B on the Columbia River—but when it happened the third morning, his gut told him something was wrong, and he insisted on taking Crystal to a nearby clinic.

"I'm fine," she told him, blowing out a breath of impatience as they pulled into the parking lot.

Luke grunted. It was still winter and flu season and all. Besides, she'd been pale and shaky for the last few days. If she was sick, by God, he would get her help. He sure as hell wasn't going to blow this off, no matter how much it annoyed her.

"Let's go," he said, turning off the engine and opening his door.

She frowned at him. "You're bossy."

"Damn straight I am." He came around to help her down from the cab of his truck and put his arm around her waist for support. Naturally, this made her frown darken.

"I'm not helpless."

"Was I saying you were helpless?" Still, he opened the clinic door for her.

Thankfully the clinic wasn't busy, and a nurse took them back to an examination room right away. "How are you feeling this morning?" she said with supreme chirpiness.

"Fine." Crystal even shot her a smile.

He glowered at her. "You're not fine. Don't tell her you're fine. Tell her you threw up this morning." He turned to the nurse. "She threw up this morning. And yesterday. And the day before that."

"It's just nerves," Crystal insisted to the nurse. "I feel better after I've, um, evacuated."

"Nerves?" The nurse quirked an eyebrow.

"We just got married," Crystal explained.

"Oh! Congratulations."

When it looked like the two were about to embark on a wedding-related conversation of some kind, he thought it would be wise to interrupt. Those conversations, once they got started, could be endless. "I'm thinking it could be the flu. Can we check her temperature?"

"Sure." The nurse sent him a knowing grin, then pulled out a thermometer and swiped it across Crystal's forehead. "Mmm-hmm," she said as she read the results.

"Well?" he said, maybe a little more eagerly than was necessary.

"Ninety-eight-point-five."

He nearly deflated. "She felt warmer than that," he muttered.

As the nurse took the rest of Crystal's vitals, they chatted and Luke fretted. "So have you ever felt sick like this before?" the nurse asked.

Crystal shrugged. "Just once. But it it's not that." She glanced at Luke so he took her hand.

"And when was that?"

Crystal paled. Luke tightened his hold. "Um. I was pregnant with Jack."

"I see. Have you taken a pregnancy test yet?"

"No," Crystal said, putting a hand to her head. "I didn't… We can't possibly be… I mean, we just…"

"Well, everything else looks normal, so let's try that, shall we?"

"Go on, honey," he urged her when she sent him a dazed look. Hell, it couldn't hurt. If she were pregnant— God, how amazing would that be? A zephyr of excitement and anticipation whipped through him. "I'll wait right here."

At long last, the door to the little room opened and Crystal stepped through. She held a small white wand in her fist. She said nothing, just stared at him.

"Hon?" he prompted. He tried to sound blasé, but his heart pounded like a bass drum.

"It's positive, Luke."

"Oh. Oh, God." He stared at her as realization swept through him like a raging river. His knees went weak. He plopped down on the chair. "Oh, God."

"Oh, God," she agreed, sitting next to him.

She was pale. Her brow was furrowed. "Are you okay?" he had to ask. *Please let her be happy. Please.*

Relief sluiced through him when her face split in a grin. "We're going to have a baby, Luke."

"A baby." Such a small word for such great joy. It was the most wonderful thing in the world, when Luke had believed things were as wonderful as they could get.

What a blessing.

What a gift.

"God, I love you," he said, kissing her soundly.

"Yeah," she said with a glowing grin. "I know."

In the end Luke and Crystal cut their honeymoon short—happily so—and headed straight back to Butterscotch Ridge to share the news. She stared out at the endless drifts of snow with a smile on her face as she planned their future.

Luke shot her a glance. "You okay?"

She laughed. "So happy." She reached over and threaded her fingers with his. "How do you suppose Jack will take it?" The thought was her only worry. Jack had been an only child his whole life. A baby would change his world from top to bottom.

"He's a great kid. He'll be fine."

"We're going to have a baby." It was a magical

thing to say. The words alone sent ripples of happiness dancing over her soul. "Would you rather have a boy or a girl?"

Luke grinned. "I don't really care, as long as it's healthy."

"Me, too." She shot him a glance. "Are you as happy as I am?"

"Me?" He was quiet for a minute. "Crystal, honey, I'm over the moon."

She grinned at him. "This time next year, we'll be a family of four."

They drove in silence for a while, processing the depth of emotion that threatened to wash them away in a wave of pure elation. As they turned onto the Stirling Ranch drive, Luke cleared his throat. "So," he said. "Are we ready to tell Jack?"

Crystal blinked. "We?"

He glanced at her, and offered a conciliatory smile. "We'll do it together." He reached a hand out to her and she took it. "Like everything from now on, we'll do it together. As a team."

And they did.

* * * * *

WE HOPE YOU ENJOYED
THIS BOOK FROM

Believe in love. Overcome obstacles. Find happiness.

Relate to finding comfort and strength in the
support of loved ones and enjoy the journey
no matter what life throws your way.

6 NEW BOOKS AVAILABLE EVERY MONTH!